# CITY OF
# DARKNESS

**The Best in Today's Fiction . . .
for Today's Readers**

*Finder*
by Emma Bull

*Briar Rose*
by Jane Yolen

*Wildside*
by Steven Gould

*Sister Light, Sister Dark*
by Jane Yolen

*City of Darkness*
by Ben Bova

*The One-Armed Queen*
by Jane Yolen

*Dogland*
by Will Shetterly

*White Jenna*
by Jane Yolen

*War for the Oaks*
by Emma Bull

# CITY OF DARKNESS

## BEN BOVA

**TOR**

A TOM DOHERTY ASSOCIATES BOOK
NEW YORK

This is a work of fiction. All the characters and events portrayed in this book are either products of the author's imagination or are used fictitiously.

CITY OF DARKNESS

Copyright © 2003 by Ben Bova
All rights reserved, including the right to reproduce this book, or portions thereof, in any form.

*Previously published by Berkley Books*

A Tor Book
Published by Tom Doherty Associates, LLC
175 Fifth Avenue
New York, NY 10010

www.tor.com

Tor® is a registered trademark of Tom Doherty Associates, LLC.

ISBN 0-765-34361-4
EAN 978-0765-3436-1

First Tor Teen edition: March 2004

Printed in the United States of America

0  9  8  7  6  5  4  3  2

*To Susan, Amy, Tony, Stu*
*and all the NESFAs*

*Oh beautiful for patriot's dream*
*That sees beyond the years,*
*Thine alabaster cities gleam*
*Undimmed by human tears . . .*

"America the Beautiful"
Katherine Lee Bates (1911)


*Save the people!*
*Save the children!*
*Save the country!*
*NOW!*

"Save the Country"
Recorded by the Fifth Dimension (1970)

"nd the girls . . . wow!" said Ron Morgan.

"What about them?"

"How'd they look?"

Ron was sitting on the edge of the swimming pool, his feet swishing in the heated water. It was a cool, clear, late summer night. Eight of his buddies were clustered around him on the astroturf of the back yard. The only lights were the pool's underwater lamps, which threw strange shimmering shadows on the boys' faces.

"New York City girls are something else," Ron told them. "It's hard to describe. They're not prettier than the girls here at home, but . . ."

"But *what*?" Jimmy Glenn squeaked in his cracking voice. "Don't hang us up!"

"Well . . ." Ron searched for the best words. "They sort of— well, for one thing, they dress differently. Sharp. Like they want to be seen. I guess that's it. They know what it's all about, and they like it!"

"Not like Sally-Ann."

"That dimwit."

Ron went on, "They want guys to notice them. They even stare right back at you when you look them over."

One of the boys laughed. "Dude, I'm going to talk my dad into taking me to New York City before the summer's over."

"Your dad must be okay, Ron—taking you to the City."

"Hey, he likes it too, you know," Ron answered.

"Is the City really that great, Ron? I mean, for real?"

Ron smiled. He had an even-featured, good-looking face. Like all the boys around the pool, his teeth were straight, his eyes were clear, his lean teen-aged body was strong and unblemished, thanks to a lifetime of carefully regulated diet, vitamins, exactly eight hours' sleep each night, and the school's physical fitness programs.

"It's the only city they open up, isn't it?" Ron answered with a question. "All the other cities have been closed down, haven't they?"

"There's still a couple cities open out West," said Reggie Gilmore.

"They're just little ones."

"San Francisco's not so little!"

"Yeah, but Mr. Armbruster in Social Consciousness class said the Government was going to close down San Francisco next year, too. They had an epidemic there this summer."

"It's a lot better out here in the Tracts," one of the boys said. "We're safer and healthier."

"You get an A for social consciousness, Leroy!"

All the boys laughed, except Leroy, who knew that all believed the same way he did, even though they kidded him for admitting it openly.

"New York is wild," Ron said, taking over the conversation again. "The streets are jammed with people. You can hardly walk. Stores everyplace. Not just shopping centers, but all over the place! You can buy anything from clothes to stereo TVs without walking more than a block."

"But it's real unsanitary, isn't it?"

Ron nodded. "Absolutely! The streets are filthy. How can you keep them clean, with so many people pushing around everyplace? And they've got old-fashioned gas-burning cars in the streets. The pollution! And the noise! The cars and horns and people talking and shouting . . . it's crazy. No wonder they only keep the City open during summer vacation. It's too unsanitary for people to live in New York all year 'round."

"Where do all the people go, after the summer's over?"

"Back to the Tracts, dumbhead! Just like Ron and his dad, right?"

"That's right," Ron said. "They close the City after Labor Day and everybody goes back to their homes. Then the next spring they open it up again, for the vacation season."

"Man, I'd like to spend a summer there!"

"Can't. They only allow you to stay two weeks, at the most."

"Two weeks, then. Cheez!"

The boys were silent for a few moments, and the night was silent with them. No crickets, no mosquitos, no sounds of life at all. Nothing except the darkness and the softest humming of the methane-fueled generator, which provided electric power once the sun went down.

Ron splashed at the water with his feet.

"The girls are really terrific, huh?"

With a laugh, he answered, "More than that. They've got something they call bedicabs driving around along the streets. With a meter and everything."

"What's that for?" Jimmy asked.

The other guys hooted at him.

"Ohhh!" Jimmy finally got it. "Okay, so I'm a slow learner. Do they charge by the mile or the hour?"

After they quieted down again, Ron resumed, "When you leave Manhattan Dome and start out for the train station to go home, they put you on a special bus—it's sort of like an ambulance. They take off all your clothes and get rid of them. Then they make you shower and they cleanse you with all sorts of special stuff. You have to stick a tube down your nose and all the way into your lungs—"

"Yuchk!"

"Yeah, but you've got to get rid of the carcinogens you breathed in while you were in the City. And the germs. You pick up enough germs to start an epidemic back home, the medic told us."

"Well, cancel my trip. I'm not going through *that*."

"I am," Ron said. "I'm going back to New York City before they close it for the winter."

"You are?"

"Yep. And this time I'm going alone, without my dad. There are a lot of things to see and do that he wouldn't let me into. He always thinks he knows best . . . treats me like a kid."

Jimmy asked, "Does your father know you're going back alone?"

"No. And don't anybody tell on me, either."

They were still talking about New York City when the ten o'clock whistle went off.

"Damn!"

"Curfew time already?"

"I bet those security cops ring it early on us."

"They can't. It's automatic."

The boys got up slowly, grumbling. Ron pulled himself to his feet.

Jimmy came over beside him and asked softly, "Are you really going back to New York City?"

Nodding, Ron said, "You bet. I don't know how I'm going to do it, but I'm going."

"There's only a week or so left before Labor Day. Don't they close the City after that?"

"Yep."

"Wish I could go, too."

"Come on along!" Ron said, enthusiastically. "It'd be terrific, the two of us."

"Naw, I can't. My folks wouldn't let me."

"Don't tell them!"

Jimmy scuffed at the astroturf with a bare foot.

"They'd kill me when I got back. Naw . . . I just can't."

Ron didn't know what to say. He just stood there.

"Well . . . g'night," Jimmy said.

Ron shrugged at him.

The boys filed through the back gate in the fence that surrounded Ron's house. They fanned out, each heading for his own house. All the houses on the long curving broad quiet street were the same. Each had a broad back lawn of astroturf with a swimming pool and the same low, imitation-wood fences. In each of the houses, the parents sat watching TV, like good citizen consumers.

The Tract houses went on, street after street, row after row, for as far as Ron knew. The only break in their ranks was the big shopping center, where all the fathers worked in offices on the upper floors of the store buildings. The train station was next to the shopping center, underground, beneath the parking lot. The train ran through a deep tunnel, so Ron never saw where the Tracts ended and the City began.

Ron stood beside the pool for a long while and looked up at the stars. The sky was completely clear of clouds. The Weather Control Force wouldn't start the nightly rain for another couple of hours. Up there now in the blackness he could see sparkling Vega and brilliant Altair. And there was Deneb, at the tail of the Swan—the stars of the Swan stretched halfway across the summer sky in a long, graceful cross, slim and beautiful.

*If only Dad could see how beautiful it all is*, Ron thought. *If only . . .*

Then he remembered the National Exams. The tests that settled what your career would be. The tests that fixed the pattern of the rest of your life. If you did poorly, the chances were that they would put you in the Social Services, or worse, in the Army. But if you did well—incredibly well—maybe you could get to spend your whole life studying the stars.

They'd tell him how he scored on the tests tomorrow.

Tomorrow was going to be The Day.

Tomorrow.

A movement of light caught his eye. Far down the row of houses, a silent patrol car was gliding along the emptied street. The security patrol, making certain that nobody was out past curfew.

Ron shook his head and headed for the house. He knew that his parents were watching TV: Dad in his den and Mother in her bedroom. Mother never felt very strong, so they seldom had friends over. Ron went straight up to his room without bothering either of his parents.

*Before they close the City down, I'm going back to New York*, he told himself again. *No matter what the National Exam results are, I'm going back.*

**R**on woke up.

His eyes snapped open and he was awake. Not groggy at all. Eyes wide open, mind clear and sharp. He could hear the morning music and news coming from his alarm stereo, the newscaster's soft voice purring along in cadence to the "easy listening" music. The sun was streaming through his bedroom window. Very faintly, Ron could hear the water circulating in the solar-powered pumps between his bedroom ceiling and the roof.

A moment ago he had been sleeping, dreaming something ugly and scary. Now he was so fully awake that he couldn't even remember what his dream was about. He lay on his back, staring up at the ceiling. He had painted patterns of stars up there on the blue paneling: Orion, the Dippers, the Lion—

*The Exam results*, he suddenly recalled. *Today's The Day!*
Forever Day.

He got out of bed and walked quietly to the sanitary stall. The needle-spray shower felt good. The hot-air blower felt even better. Ron looked at his face in the stall's mirror. He had never been very happy about his face. The nose was too big and the eyes were too small. Ordinary brown eyes. Brown hair, too. Just ordinary.

He had seen a few guys in New York with long hair, really long and flowing. It looked weird at first. Ron stared at his own short-clipped hair. Nice and trim. Everybody wore it that way at home. Easy to keep clean. Sanitary. Ordinary.

He wondered how it would look if it were long, long enough to flow over his shoulders. Then he pictured what his father would say. Or scream.

There was some dark brown fuzz on his chin, so Ron rubbed in a palmful of shaving powder and rinsed it all off. Now even his mother would agree that he looked clean and sanitary.

Pulling on a t-shirt and shorts, Ron noticed how quiet the house was. The alarm stereo had shut off, of course, as soon as he'd gotten up from the bed. *It's early*, he told himself. His mother stayed in bed most of the time; doctor's orders, she said. Dad didn't have to leave for his office for another hour. Ron slid his feet into his plastic sandals and went downstairs.

His father was already in the kitchen, sitting at the breakfast counter with a cup of steaming coffee in front of him, watching the morning news on the wall TV.

"You're up early," said Ron's father. "Nervous?"

Nodding, Ron answered, "Guess so."

Mr. Morgan was nearly fifty years old. His hair was gray and thin, with a bald spot showing no matter how he combed it. Ron had seen photos of his father when he had been much younger—he had been tall and trim and he was grinning happily in those pictures. Now he was heavy, almost fat. And he seldom smiled.

*Someday I'll be just like him*, Ron thought. *Rich and overweight and old. Unless . . .*

The wall TV showed a handful of soldiers walking slowly, painfully, through some jungle growth. They looked all worn out: shoulders sagging, mouths hanging open, shirts dark with sweat, eyes red and puffy. One of them had a blood-soaked bandage wrapped around his middle. His arms were draped over the shoulders of two buddies, who were half carrying, half dragging him along. All but two of the soldiers on the screen were black. The only black people Ron had ever seen were on TV.

The TV newscaster was saying: ". . . and only sixteen Americans were lost in this skirmish near the Amazon River delta. Fifty-four enemy dead were counted and verified, and . . ."

He sounded so damned *cheerful!* Ron stared at the soldiers. He knew they were his own age, or maybe a year older, at most. But they looked like old men—old, old men who had seen death so often and so close that nothing else mattered to them.

The TV picture suddenly snapped off. Ron felt himself jerk back a little in surprise. His father had turned it off.

"You don't have to worry about things like that," his father said.

Ron looked at him. "If I didn't do well in the Exams—"

"You won't be drafted, don't worry," Mr. Morgan insisted. "Even if you flunked the Exams, I can buy your way out of the draft. The draft's not for kids like you, anyway. It's for those poor slobs—those bums who couldn't hold down a decent job even if you handed it to them on a platinum platter."

"But—"

"Don't worry about it, I'm telling you." The older man's voice went up a notch, which meant he wasn't going to listen to anything Ron had to say on the subject.

"Okay, sure." For a moment Ron stared at the now-dead TV screen. He could still see the young-old soldiers.

Then he went around the breakfast counter and pulled a package from the freezer. The cold metal foil made his fingers tingle. He put the package in the microwave cooker and thirty seconds later out slid the package, sizzling hot. Ron grabbed it and put it in front of his father quickly, before the heat could get to his fingers.

Mr. Morgan peeled back the metal foil to reveal steaming eggs, pancakes, and sausages. He looked up at his son. "Where's yours?"

"I'm not hungry," Ron said.

His father huffed. "You ought to eat something. Get me some juice, will you? At least have a glass of milk. You shouldn't start the day on an empty stomach."

Ron got the juice and the milk. He drank half a glass of ice-cold milk and watched his father eating. But he kept glancing at the clock on the wall, next to the TV screen. *The call will come at nine o'clock*, he knew. *They always call at nine sharp.*

An hour and a half to go, and the seconds-counter on the

digital clock was crawling like a wounded soldier dragging himself through jungle mud.

"I . . . I'm going out to the garage," Ron said.

His father stared at him a moment, then said, "All right. I'll call you when the Examiner phones."

"You're not going to work today?"

With a tight smile, Ron's father said, "I'll wait until the Examiner calls."

Ron nodded and headed for the back door.

It was cool and pleasant outside. The night's rain had washed the sky a clean and cloudless blue.

The garage was really more of a workshop than anything else. The family electric car always stayed out on the driveway where the neighbors could see how big and new it was. It took so much electrical power to run it that Mr. Morgan had to keep it plugged in to the garage's special power-charger all night. Once he had backed out of the driveway without disconnecting the cable. It snapped across the windshield like a whip, crazing it into a million spiderwebs of cracks. Mr. Morgan spent an hour hopping up and down on the driveway next to his car, screaming at everybody about everything except his own forgetfulness.

Ron had fixed the cable and the plug. He had also wanted to try to put in the new windshield, but his father wouldn't let him. Mr. Morgan took the car to a repair shop, where they charged him six times what Ron thought the job was worth. But Ron did change the socket in the car, so that it would automatically disengage and release the cable when the car began to move.

"That's pretty good, son," Mr. Morgan had said, with genuine astonishment in his voice.

So Ron clanked around in the garage workshop for more than an hour. He deliberately avoided looking at his wristwatch. Instead, he worked on the electronic image booster that he was building for his telescope. It would allow the instrument to pick out stars that were far too faint for an unboosted telescope to register. With this electronics package, Ron's telescope would be almost the equal of the big reflector in the school's observatory.

"Ron!" His father's voice.

He suddenly felt hot and cold at the same time. His guts seemed to go rigid, and he could hear the blood pounding in his ears. Stiffly, Ron walked back to the house. Through the back door into the kitchen, across the dining area, and into the family room.

His father was sitting on the big plastic sofa. The full-wall TV screen was connected to the phone, so the Examiner's face looked out at them, huge and frightening.

But he was smiling. The Examiner had a thin face, with absolutely white hair that was cropped so close to his slightly square skull that it looked like baby fuzz. But his face wasn't a baby's. It was lined and lean and leathery.

But he was smiling!

"Ahh . . . and this is our young man," said the Examiner.

He hadn't been smiling when he'd handed out the test sheets to Ron and the other sixteen-year-olds. Nor had he smiled when they had left the Exams, eight grueling hours later.

"Ron, you kept the Examiner waiting," his father snapped.

"I'm sorry . . . I was out in the workshop . . ." *But you knew that*, Ron thought.

The Examiner said, "Perfectly all right, although I am rather pressed for time. Ronald Morgan, I have the pleasure of announcing that you scored in the top three percent of the National Exams."

Ron felt the breath gush out of him. He hadn't realized he had been holding his breath. His father broke into a broad grin and looked up at him happily.

"Your scores were especially good in the mechanical arts and electronics. Math was a little low, but still in the highest ten percentile. All in all, one of the best Exams it's been my pleasure to score this year. Congratulations."

"Um . . . er . . . thank you, sir."

"Marvelous, son. Marvelous."

"Now then," the Examiner went on, "you are in the happy position of being qualified to choose the Career vector you desire. You are obviously too valuable a man for service in the Armed Forces—unless you choose to volunteer for officer training. With your Exam results, you could be commissioned in the Army, Navy, or Space Forces quite easily."

Ron's father said, "I don't think—"

"No, no, no," said the Examiner. "The decision must not be made right now. You must take your time and decide by the end of the month. You must think over many different sides of the problem."

"Of course. Excuse me."

Turning his gaze back to Ron, the Examiner went on, "In addition to the Service vector, the next choice of Career vector is in the Business community. You can enter the Business college of your choice, with these Exam results behind you. There are several fine schools in this State that are free. There are even better private Business schools, if you so choose."

Ron nodded.

"The final choice open to you is the University vector. Your high scores in science and the mechanical arts show that you would enjoy a career in science or engineering. You'd need to work a little harder on your math, of course."

"Yes," Ron agreed.

"There are very few career openings in the sciences, you must realize. Only a young man with as brilliant an Exam as yours can even think of trying for the sciences. On the other hand, there is a great need for engineers—men who can make machines work properly. If I were making a recommendation, that's what I would pick for you."

The Examiner stopped talking and looked at Ron. Not knowing what to say, Ron simply mumbled, "Thank you, sir," again.

"Very good," the Examiner said. "Well . . . talk it over. Think about it very carefully. Remember that the choice you make will determine your Career vector for life. This is the most important choice you will ever make, young man. Good luck. I will expect to hear from you by the first . . . no, no, there's the Labor Day holiday. I will expect to hear from you on the Tuesday after Labor Day."

"Thank you," Mr. Morgan said.

The TV screen faded into grayness.

"Son, I'm proud of you!" Mr. Morgan pulled himself up from the sofa and stood before his son, with his hand outstretched. Ron grasped it, grinning and feeling a little sheepish.

His father pumped Ron's hand hard. "You've done very well. Very well indeed."

"Thanks, Dad."

"Come on, let's go up and tell your mother."

Mrs. Morgan was quiet and frail. She lived on pills and long talks with doctors on the TV phone. She seldom left her bedroom. When Ron and his father entered her bedroom, she was sitting up in bed, her lounging robe buttoned up to the neck. She smiled and nodded when they told her of the Examiner's call. Then she called Ron over to her side and hugged him.

"I knew you would make it, Ronnie dear," she said.

After a few moments of her fussing over Ron, Mr. Morgan took over and pulled him away from her. He towed Ron by the arm out of her bedroom and into his own den. It was a darkly paneled room, part office and part hideaway. Mr. Morgan closed the door firmly and pointed to the chair in front of his desk.

"Sit down, son."

Ron sat while his father went behind the desk and pulled a little booklet from one of the drawers.

"This is from Getty College, where I went to school," Mr. Morgan said, sliding the booklet across the desk toward Ron. "I knew you'd do well in the Exams. I've already enrolled you in Getty's business school—the same course that I had as a freshman!"

And now Ron knew why he had been scared. It wasn't that he had been afraid of flunking the Exams, of going into the Army to fight in South America. It was this. He was afraid of his father.

"Dad . . ." His voice was so low that he could barely hear himself. "Dad . . . I, uh . . . I don't know if I want to go to business school. Maybe I ought to try science. The Examiner said—"

"Science?" Mr. Morgan's face went hard. His brows pulled together in a frown. "Science? What good is that? Spend the rest of your life in some dumb university, teaching kids useless stuff? No, that's not for you."

"But it's what I like best. The Examiner said—"

"I was there!" His father's voice got louder. "I heard what he said. He said he'd recommend engineering, not science. But I'm telling you that you're going into business. That's where the money is."

"But I—"

"Don't argue! I'm your father and you'll do as I say!"

Ron said, "It's my life, Dad."

"And you think you're old enough to run it for yourself? You're only a sixteen-year-old snot! Who the hell do you think you are to turn your nose up at a business career? Nine-tenths of the kids in this Tract would sell their sisters for the chance to go to Getty! You just don't know what you're doing."

Before Ron could think of anything for an answer, his father went on, but in a gentler voice, "Listen, son, I really know a lot more about the world than you do. The business career is best, believe me. Once you—"

Ron stared at the carpet and shook his head.

His father pounded a fist on the desk so hard that the desk lamp tumbled over. Ron jerked back and looked up at the old man—he was red-faced and snarling.

"You're going to Getty whether you like it or not!" he shouted.

*No I'm not*, Ron said to himself. *I'm going to run away. I'll go to New York!*

**I** t was easy.

So easy that Ron could hardly believe it. It took him all week to work up the nerve. Then, on Saturday morning, while his father was out with his usual golfing foursome, he told his mother that he was going to spend the weekend with some of his friends who lived in the next housing Tract, a few miles away.

"Don't go on the freeway with your bike, Ronnie dear. Stay on the secondary roads—they're safer."

That's all she said.

Ron went up to his room and put on a clean one-piece zipsuit. *I can get throwaway clothes in New York*, he thought. *Don't have to carry anything else with me.* He took his credit card and all the cash he had in the house, about thirty dollars. He walked his power bike out of the garage, started its tiny electric motor, and hummed down the driveway and into the street.

Fifteen minutes later he was in a sleek air train, whizzing along at three hundred miles per hour through a deep tunnel. The bike was locked in a stall at the train terminal. He would pick it up on the way home.

The train was packed. Ron sat in a four-passenger compartment, but six people were jammed in there. All adults, all men his father's age. They all looked grim. They were going to New York to have one last good time before the summer ended, even if it hurt.

Nobody talked. The only sound was the noise of air whistling past between the outside skin of the train and the tunnel wall. The compartment was painted a pleasant bright green, with clever little decorations spotted here and there along its paneled walls. There were no windows and nothing to see outside except the bare tunnel wall rocketing past. There was a blank TV screen on the partition wall in front of Ron, but he didn't feel like watching TV. Besides, he got the feeling that his five cramped compartment-mates would object if he turned on one of the shows that he liked.

Ron saw his own face reflected in the dead screen. He was frowning. Thinking about what was going to happen when he returned home. It was Labor Day weekend. He had today, Sunday, and most of Monday to be in the City. Monday night he'd have to go back home—and face his father.

*Okay, so I'll go to business school. I can always make astronomy my hobby.* But he hated it. He hated being forced into something he didn't want to do. He hated having to give up what he wanted most. And he hated the feeling that there was nothing he could do about it.

*Well, you've got this weekend*, he told himself. *Make the most of it.*

It was only a little past noon when the train pulled into Grand Central Station. Stepping out of the train's clean plastic shell and onto the station platform was like stepping from an art museum into a riot.

The noise hit Ron first. There were thousands of people bustling around the station platform, all of them talking, shouting, arguing at once. Policemen in black uniforms and white hard helmets were directing people into lines that surged up moving stairs. People were struggling with luggage. One old man—Ron's father's age—was screaming red-faced at a porter in a ragged uniform who had dropped a suitcase. It had popped open and all sorts of clothing were scattered across the filthy platform floor. People were trampling over the clothes, paying absolutely no attention to the man's yowls.

Ron got into line behind a fat woman who was clutching a six-year-old girl by the wrist. The child was scared and whimpering.

"I don't like it here, Mommy. I want to go home."

The woman jerked the child's arm hard enough to lift the kid off her feet. Bending down to push her puffy face into her daughter's, she said: "Listen, you little brat. It cost plenty to get here and I didn't have to bring you in the first place. Now you behave or I'll sell you to the first meat grinder I see."

The child's eyes went wide with terror. For a moment she

tried hard not to cry, but it was too much for her. She burst into a wild, high-pitched scream. Tears poured down her cheeks and past her open mouth.

"Shut up!" her mother hissed at her, glancing around at the crowd. Ron saw that everybody on the moving stairway was looking the other way, trying hard to ignore them.

Ron wanted to bend down and tell the little girl that she didn't have to be afraid. But he didn't know if he should or not. So he just stood there while the child cried and the mother glared and threatened. He felt confused and sad, and a little guilty about not doing anything to help the child.

At the top of the long moving stairway the crowd was broken into smaller groups by still more policemen and set up into dozens of lines. The woman and her child disappeared somewhere in the confused, chaotic mass of people. Ron found that the line he was shunted into wasn't terribly long, only about twenty people ahead of him. But it moved very slowly.

It was hot and Ron felt sweaty. The noise that pounded in from everywhere in this huge cavern of a room made it feel even hotter. Echoes bounced off the vast ceiling, high overhead. It felt as if all the people in the world were in there, shouting at each other and heating up the station to the boiling point.

Ron leaned out to see around the people in front of him. The line ended at an entrance booth. He remembered the entrance booths from the time before.

People jostled and grumbled and looked at their watches and wiped their brows and complained. But the line moved slowly, slowly. Finally Ron was standing at the booth. He slid his credit card and ID card across the counter to a tired-looking man with narrow, bloodshot eyes and tight, thin lips.

"Fullamnt?" the man mumbled.

"What?" Ron asked.

Looking disgusted, the man said more slowly, "Full amount? Ya want the full amounta cash dat the credit card covers? Dat's two towsan dollahs."

"Oh." Ron finally understood. "Yes, two thousand dollars, please."

The man touched a button and a neatly, wrapped package of bills popped up from a little trapdoor in the counter.

"Y' alone?" the man asked.

"Yessir."

"How old are ya?"

Ron suddenly noticed the sign on the back wall of the man's booth: CHILDREN UNDER EIGHTEEN NOT ADMITTED UNLESS ACCOMPANIED BY PARENT OR GUARDIAN.

"Uh . . . I'm eighteen."

The man's sour face turned even more sour. "Fifty bucks," he said.

"What?"

"Fifty," he pronounced carefully. "Gimme—give me fifty dollahs."

Ron tried to remember if his father had paid anything at the entrance booth. "But why?"

"Look kid, you ain't eighteen. Ya want me to believe you're eighteen, gimme fifty. Otherwise, go home. Now c'mon, you're holdin' up the line."

Ron blinked at him. "But that's illegal! You can't—"

"Ya wanna get in or ya wanna go home? C'mon, there's lotsa people waitin'."

Ron looked around. The people in line were glaring at him, angry, hot, and impatient. There was a policeman nearby, tall and official-looking in his uniform and helmet. But he was carefully looking in the other direction.

Ron tore the plastic wrapping off his package of bills and pulled out a fifty. He slid it across the counter.

"Welcome t' Fun City," said the man in the booth in a flat, totally automatic way.

The little gate at the far end of the booth clicked open and Ron stepped through. He was now officially in New York City.

"Watch it!"

A porter in an electric wagon piled high with luggage zipped past him. Ron had to jump back to get out of the way.

Ron pushed through the crowd and made it outside to the street. The throngs here were even thicker and noisier, pushing and shouldering along the sidewalk. Everyone was going someplace. Someplace important, too, from the busy looks on their faces. At the curb was a line of cabs, and people poured into them. Cars were charging down the street. They pulled up short when the traffic light turned red, then roared for the next light as soon as it flashed green again. Bumpers banged but nobody seemed to care or even notice.

These cars weren't the safe, quiet electrics that were used in the Tracts. These smoked and went *vrooom!* when they started up. *Unsanitary*, Ron told himself. *They make a terrible amount of pollution.* Still, he yearned to drive one.

Down the street he rushed. He couldn't walk slowly because the crowd pushed him along, move, move, move. Doesn't matter where you're going or why. Just keep moving or they'll trample over you.

A little old lady with a sweet smile and an umbrella passed him, heading the other way. She was holding a leash that was attached to the collar of the biggest dog Ron had ever seen. Walking a dog, on a public street! In the daytime! Back home, you couldn't take a dog out on the street at all. You could only walk him in the park, or on your own property, and then only at night.

It wasn't until after the lady with the dog had passed that Ron thought about her umbrella. It took him a minute to figure out what the odd-looking thing was. Back home, with the Weather Control Force in charge of everything, you always knew well in advance when it was going to rain. And here, under Manhattan Dome, why would anyone need an umbrella at all?

He glanced upward. Yes, the Dome was still up there. He could see its gray steel framework, like a giant spiderweb, far, far above. It was almost lost in the haze of smog that hung above the street.

Two blocks down the street Ron found a clothing store. The windows looked great. Real live models walking up and down inside the windows, talking to one another, tossing a ball around, laughing and waving to the crowd. A bunch of people had gathered in front of the window to watch them. Ron fought his way past the stream of people walking down the street and got to the edge of the crowd at the window. He was tall enough to see over the heads of most of them.

The girls were fantastic! Shorts and little sleeveless tops that barely covered their figures. Not at all like the girls back at the Tracts, with their shapeless prefaded sloppy clothes and their constant challenging in the classroom and the athletic field. Ron grinned at these girls and they smiled right back. Every few minutes a new model would come into the window and one of the others would leave. *To change into a new outfit*, Ron guessed.

The window must have been soundproofed, because Ron could see the models moving their lips, talking, but he couldn't hear them at all. The people in the crowd were yelling things to them, but they paid no attention. Some of the things that the grown men said to those girls . . . Ron was surprised at first, then he got sore. *Dirty old cruds*, he said to himself.

Ron began to notice the clothes that the boys were modeling. Wild. Leather, and macho-looking real metal zippers. Snug-fitting. Boots. Stripes. Glancing down at his own loose, pale green zipsuit, Ron started to feel like a real country dork. A plastic imitation. He nodded once to himself and then pushed his way through the crowd to the store's entrance.

Inside it was much quieter. And cool. The air felt pleasant and clean. It even smelled good.

And there were human people in there to wait on you! Not the automatic machines like they had in the stores back home.

Instead of talking to a dumb computer, there were people here to listen to you and make suggestions.

They were men, mostly. Some of them were young, in their twenties. But most of them were older. Gray hair, getting heavy, but smiling and ready to help a dumb kid from the Tracts.

They measured Ron: arms, legs, chest, waist, neck. They fussed all around him and brought out some of the models from the window to show him different kinds of outfits. A few of the girls from the window hung around, too, watching and smiling.

When Ron strutted out of the store, he was dressed in a black polyester suit with silver emblems on the shoulders. His boots were real synthetic leather. He felt about eighteen feet tall.

He was also three hundred dollars lighter. Under his arm he clutched a plastic box that contained another entire outfit, plus his old green zipsuit, wrinkled and tossed in only for the trip back home.

*Now I look like a real New Yorker*, he told himself as he strode down the street. Everyone else was dressed in very ordinary clothes. Tourists. Vistors. Ron noticed how they all stared at his outfit. He grinned. He pictured himself as an Executive, one of the men who used to live high up in a skyscraper before the City was closed and evacuated. His grin widened.

Further down the street was a movie theater. It was showing old-time films. The big signs flashing above the entrance said: MURDER! FIGHTS! WAR! SEX! There were no theaters at home. TV was everything, and kids weren't allowed to watch anything more exciting than the six o'clock news.

It cost another twenty dollars, but Ron didn't care. He sailed right into the theater. It was completely dark inside, and he bumped into several chairs and people before he could find an empty seat for himself.

For four hours he watched exactly what the signs outside had promised. Blood and fighting. Beautiful girls and handsome men. War and all sorts of thrilling adventures. One of the films starred two guys named Redman and Newford, or something like that. They were terrific.

People got up and left and other people came in. Ron ignored them, his eyes locked on the screen. He watched people shoot each other, make love, fight wars that were much more exciting and fun than the warfare in South America. He saw doctors, policemen, killers, and each girl was better-looking than the last one.

Somebody stepped on his foot.

"Oh! Sorry."

Ron looked up at the person who had done it. She came into the aisle and sat in the seat next to his. In the changing, colored light from the movie screen, Ron could see that she was about his own age. And kind of pretty.

"I'm awful sorry. Hope I didn't hurt your foot."

"No, it's all right."

She didn't say anything else, and Ron went back to watching the screen. But he kept glancing at her. She was *very* pretty. And dressed sharp, too. He wanted to talk to her, to say something, anything, just to start a conversation. But his tongue was frozen. He didn't know where to begin.

He was watching her now, not the movie. She was looking

straight ahead, at the screen, and smiling slightly.

*She doesn't even know I'm sitting next to her.* Ron felt miserable.

Then all of a sudden she turned to him. "Live'n th' City?"

Ron's throat was so dry it took him three tries to say, "Uh . . . no. I'm from Vermont."

"Oh. From yer clothes, I thoughtcha lived here." She spoke fast, blurring her words together. Ron had to listen hard to understand her, especially with the movie's sound track blaring at them quadraphonically.

"No . . . no . . . I'm just here . . . for a few days."

She nodded and smiled at him.

"Um . . . where are you from?"

"Noo Yawk."

"I mean, after vacation time. Where do you live then?"

She said, "Right here. I live'n th' City alla time."

"**B**ut you can't!" Ron said. "The City's closed down after this weekend. Nobody lives here after Labor Day."

"Don't let 'em kid ya," she answered.

By the time the movie was over, Ron learned that the girl's name was Sylvia Meyer. She kept insisting that she lived in New York City—in Manhattan—all the time.

"I never been Outside," Sylvia told him as they walked slowly out of the movie theater. "I was born here."

The blinking, bleary-eyed people pushing out of the theater merged into the faster-moving noisy crowd on the street. It was still bright and muggy outside, even though the Dome blocked off any direct sunshine. Cars growled and honked in the streets. People hurried along, their faces grim.

"You alone?" Sylvia asked.

Ron nodded. Out here in the better light, he could get a good look at her. She was beautiful! Long dark hair falling over her shoulders, gray eyes with a bit of an oriental look to them, and a figure that made his pulse start throbbing. She was wearing a microskirt and white boots and a kind of loose-fitting short-sleeved blouse that didn't hide anything.

"Nice rest'rant a few blocks down th' avenya," she said.

"Thanks—I was thinking I'd eat at one of the hotels. I've still got to find myself a room for the weekend."

"Cripes, you ain't got a room yet?" Sylvia shouted over the noise of the crowd. "Ya'll never get one in th' regular hotels. City's jammed."

Ron felt like an idiot. "Oh . . . then, what—"

She grinned at him. "Don't worry. I know a place where you can get a room. An' it'll be a lot cheaper'n dese big hotels they stick visitors in. Right? An' there's a good rest'rant on th' way. Right?"

Grinning back at her, Ron said, "Right. Let's go."

They fought across the stream of people walking down the street, went around a corner, and started down a cross-street. The crowd here was a little thinner, and it was easier to walk.

"Lousy tourists," Sylvia muttered. "Think they own the City."

The restaurant she led Ron to was quiet and dimly lit. It was nearly full, but it wasn't noisy and nervy like the restaurants Ron's father had gone to. Like most places in New York City, the restaurant had real live waiters. No automatic selector dials with their rows of buttons. No robot carts rolling your food tray up to your table on silent rubber wheels. Real waiters, in funny suits. Men who spoke with far-away accents and bowed and stood waiting for you to make up your mind.

Ron let Sylvia order dinner, since she knew the place. When the waiter left, she smiled at Ron and asked, "Where ya from? I don't know nothin' aboutcha."

So while they ate, Ron talked. Sylvia listened and hardly said a word. Ron jabbed on and on. It was the first time anyone had asked him to tell much about himself, and he found that he enjoyed telling the story of his life. Especially to such a fantastic-looking girl.

By the time they left the restaurant, Ron felt warm and full and happy. And also sleepy. It was dark outside now, the street lamps were on. Not all of them, Ron saw. Many of them were broken, the bulbs shattered and sharp edges of glass hanging uselessly from their sockets. There were only a few people walking on the street now, and they all seemed to be hurrying as if they were afraid that something was following them. Something terrible.

Ron shifted his package of clothes from one arm to the other. "I still don't understand how you can live here all year long when—"

Sylvia laughed. "Forget it. Don't worry about it. Hey, c'mon . . . we gotta getcha a room. Right?"

He started to follow her down a street. But it looked dark down in the direction she was heading. Glancing back over his shoulder, Ron saw that the bright lights of the main avenue seemed to be behind them.

"Wait . . . shouldn't we be going the other way?"

Sylvia reached for his free hand. "Naw—that's where all th'

tourists stay. Dose big dumps charge ya two hunnerd a night for a room th' size of a rat's nest. And they're all full-up by now. Right? C'mon down this way."

She seemed to be in a hurry.

"What's the rush?" Ron asked.

For a moment Sylvia's face looked strange. Like she wanted to tell him something but was afraid to. The light from the street lamps made everything look weird, shadowy, off-color.

"C'mon," she repeated, with a smile that was starting to look forced. "This is a great hotel. You'll like it."

Shrugging, Ron let her lead him down the street, into the deepening darkness. They crossed one avenue and started down the next block.

"Hey Sylvie."

She stopped as if she had hit a steel barrier.

Ron turned to see a guy about his own age and height step out of the shadows of a doorway. He was grinning, but there was no fun in it.

"Been waitin' fer ya," he said.

"I'm busy, Dino," Sylvia said. Her voice was suddenly flat and hard, nothing like the way she had talked to Ron.

"Yer *supposed* t'be workin'," Dino said. "I been waitin' here for a half-hour, maybe longer."

"Some other time," Sylvia said. But she didn't move.

Dino looked Ron up and down. Without taking his eyes off Ron, he asked Sylvia, "Who's th' dude? You goin' out on yer own again? You know what Al's gonna say when he finds out."

"You don't hafta tell him."

"Get ridda th' dude," Dino said, still looking at Ron.

"Flash off, Dino," Sylvia said. "I'll see ya later."

Dino pushed Ron on the chest with one hand. "Get humpin', dude. She's seen enough of you."

Ron took a half-step backward, but he could feel his anger rising. "Now wait a minute—"

"I said get humpin'!" Dino swung an open-handed slap at Ron's face.

Without thinking about it, Ron dropped the box of clothes, blocked Dino's slap, and countered with a right to his midsection. Dino's eyes popped wide and he went *"Oof!"* and folded almost in half.

But when he straightened up again there was a knife in his hand. Long and slim and glittering in the light from the street lamp.

"Dino, don't!" Sylvia screamed.

"Shuddup!" he snapped. "You get yours next."

Ron felt hot with anger. This guy was going to hurt Sylvia; he meant it. *But first he'll have to stop me.*

Strangely, Ron felt no fear. Almost like karate class back home. Calm. Even his anger was helping him to see things clearly. Dino was about his own height, yes. But he was skinny, almost frail-looking. His eyes looked weird. And he moved slowly. That slap he had aimed at Ron had been so slow that the kids in karate class would have laughed at it.

The knife made a difference. But Ron remembered his instructor's words: *Never wait for a man with a weapon to make the first move.*

So Ron faked a punch at Dino's face. Dino reacted just the way Ron expected: he jerked back a little and raised his knife hand higher. Ron kicked at his midsection with enough strength to crack a cinderblock. Dino went completely off his feet, doubled over, and landed with a thud on the sidewalk next to the building wall. He lay there in a heap of dirty, ragged clothing, not moving.

Sylvia stood by the curb, her mouth open, her eyes looking very scared.

"Quick," she said, staring at Dino's slumped form, "we better get away from here."

Ron kicked the knife into the gutter. Then he bent down and picked up his package of clothes.

"He was going to hurt you," Ron said.

She was really shaking. "He . . . he talks too much. Al wouldn't let him hurt me, an' he knows it."

"Who's Al?"

"He's—a friend of mine."

Now that the fight was over, Ron felt good. He was excited now. High. He had fought to protect her and he had won. Like Saint George against the dragon.

"Here's th' hotel," Sylvia said.

They stopped at the hotel's main doorway. It looked small and shabby. There was a little canopy over the doorway, with a row of lights around its edge. Most of the lights were missing.

Then he found that Sylvia was clinging to his arm. "Hey,"

Ron said, "you're not scared that that guy will try to follow you home and bother you again?"

"She shook her head. "I dunno. He's kinda crazy sometimes. He gets stoned and goes wild."

Without even thinking about it, Ron said, "Well look, why don't you come up to my room with me? Then you can go home later on, when it's safer."

Looking up at him, seeming very small and frightened, Sylvia said, "Okay, Ron."

They went into the lobby. There was no clerk, just an automatic sign-in machine. Sylvia held his package while Ron wrote his name on the plastic strip that stuck out of a slot in the machine. A recorded voice said: "Fifty dollars please."

Ron put a bill into the slot next to the plastic. They both got sucked inside as quickly as an eyeblink. He heard the faintest click of a camera shutter, then the same slot spit out a key that clattered into a bin in front of the machine. He reached into the bin and took the key.

He and Sylvia rode the automatic elevator up to the forty-second floor and together they walked down the long, shabby hallway, searching for the room whose number was on the key. The hallway carpet was threadbare, the walls covered with decorations that were so old you couldn't tell what they had been before they faded. The lights were dim.

He noticed that Sylvia was staying very close to him, holding his free hand and trembling.

"It's all right," he whispered to her. "He won't hurt you."

She didn't answer.

They found the right door at last and Ron unlocked it. The lights in the room went on by themselves as the door swung open. Sylvia walked in slowly and looked all around the room. Then she placed Ron's package carefully on the bench that stood at the foot of the bed.

Ron closed the door and clicked the safety latch. Turning, he saw that the room had one big bed, one night table next to it, and a long piece of low-slung furniture with some drawers in it. There was one window that you couldn't see out of, it was so grimy, one mirror above the bureau, and a wall TV screen next to it. No chairs. The only place to sit was on the bed.

It looked seedy, used. Not exactly dirty, but worn out. The room even smelled funny.

"It's not much for fifty dollars," Ron muttered to himself.

Sylvia came over to him. "Ron—you were so brave out there, against Dino. So good and strong . . ."

She slid her arms around his neck. For a flash of a second, Ron felt as if he wanted to run away. But then his arms curled around her and he was kissing her and he forgot about everything else.

on woke up slowly. For a groggy moment he didn't know where he was. Then he remembered—the hotel, New York, Sylvia.

He sat up in the bed. She was gone!

"Sylvia?" he called out.

No answer.

He padded barefoot to the tiny bathroom. The door was open and the room was dark. Nobody there.

*She's gone.*

Glancing toward the window, Ron could see that it was still dark outside. His wristwatch said two o'clock.

*She must have gone back to her own place. But where does she live? Why did she leave without telling me?*

He looked all around the room for a note, but there was nothing. Then he remembered Dino, and he started to worry.

*Maybe she left just a few minutes ago. Maybe I can catch her out on the street. She shouldn't be out alone with that nut around.*

He pulled his clothes on quickly and dashed out of the room. Down on the elevator, wishing it would go faster. Out through the empty lobby. Out onto the street.

Something hit him *thunk!* behind the ear and he went sailing slow-motion through the air. No pain, not yet. He just saw the pavement tilting sideways and rushing up closer, closer—and then he hit the cement, face and hands together. He could feel skin scraping off.

"Wha . . ."

A pair of filthy bare feet stepped in front of his eyes. Ron tried to prop himself up on one arm but somebody kicked the arm out from under him and he cracked down on the sidewalk again. He could feel his head throbbing now, and his face and hands felt raw.

"Don't bother tryin' t' get up, dude," a voice said from somewhere up above him. "Yer gonna be down there fer a long, long time."

Ron recognized the voice. Dino. He tried to roll over and get a look at him, but somebody kicked him in the ribs. And the face. And the small of the back. They were all over him, an army of them, kicking, pounding him. Pain flashed everywhere. Ron couldn't see, couldn't hear. And after what seemed like ten thousand years, he couldn't feel anything at all.

Sunlight. Bright glaring sunlight poked into his eyes painfully. No, not both eyes. Ron could open only one. The other was swollen shut.

They had dragged him over to the side of the hotel building and left him there, half sitting against the wall, half sprawled on the sidewalk.

It was daytime now, and people were walking by. Some of them glanced quickly at Ron and then just as quickly turned their heads away. Others never looked at him at all, even when they had to step over his outstretched legs. They kept their faces pointed straight ahead.

"Help . . ." Ron tried to say. But his mouth and throat were so raw that he could only make a horrible croaking sound.

With his one good eye Ron looked down at himself. His boots were gone, his clothes torn and spattered with blood. He felt numb all over. When he tried to move his legs, pain flashed through his whole body. One of his hands was swollen and blue; he couldn't move the fingers at all. His pockets had been ripped open and everything taken out of them—keys, money, credit card, ID card, everything.

Slowly, painfully, Ron tried to push himself up onto his feet. His legs wouldn't hold him.

*Got to get back . . . to the hotel . . . can't stay here . . .*

So he crawled, with pain shooting through him at every movement. Hundreds of people walked past, most of them visitors like himself. But no one stopped to help. Ron crawled along the sidewalk and pulled himself into the doorway of the hotel.

He passed out on the dusty carpet of the hotel lobby. When he awoke again, he saw that the lobby was just as empty as it had always been.

He edged over to the sign-in machine.

"Help . . . me," he moaned. "Call . . . hospital . . . police . . ."
The machine did nothing.

Ron's mind swirled. Then he realized he was dealing with a narrowly programmed machine. He took a ragged breath. "Give me . . . key . . . the key to my room." His voice sounded strange, muffled, as it came through his swollen lips.

The machine's scratchy voice tape responded, "Are you a registered guest in this hotel?"

It hurt even to breathe. Ron sat at the base of the machine and painfully nodded his head. "Yes . . . Ronald Morgan . . ."

"Your name please?" The machine asked the questions it was programmed to ask, no matter what you told it.

"Morgan . . . Ronald Morgan."

"Will you please stand directly in front of the camera so that we can compare your face against the photograph in your file. This is a protection for our registered guests, you understand."

"But I . . ." Ron knew it was useless to argue with the machine. It took several minutes and much pain, but he pulled himself to his feet, leaning heavily against the machine itself.

The camera clicked and the machine hummed to itself for a few seconds. *Can it recognize me the way I look now?* Ron wondered.

"Morgan, Ronald . . . Mr. Morgan, it is past checkout time. Checkout is eleven o'clock. You have paid for only one night, therefore you have been automatically checked out of your room."

"Checked out? But—"

"You can have your room back by paying another fifty dollars."

"They took—"

"Fifty dollars please."

"But—"

"Fifty dollars please."

Ron felt all the strength go out of him. Everything went black and he collapsed on the hotel lobby floor.

A voice woke him up. A child's voice.

The child was singing softly to himself. Ron saw that he was about six years old. His song made no sense. Either it was in a language that Ron didn't understand, or it was no language at all—just nonsense sounds. The boy's voice was high and thin. His face was very serious, as if the song was really important. His eyes were big and dark, his hair also dark, curly. His skin was a deep olive. He had skinny arms and legs, and his clothes were ragged. He was sitting on a floor littered with paper, cans and metal foil containers, rags and one old bottomless shoe. He sat with his knees tucked up close to his chin, his hands clasped around his skinny little ankles, rocking back and forth, singing.

Looking around without moving his head, Ron saw that he was in a strange room. More like a closet, it was so small. The ceiling had so many cracks in it that it looked like a road map. Huge chunks of plaster were missing from it and from the bare walls, showing crumbling lathe inside.

Ron tried to prop himself up on one elbow. His head spun

dizzily, but the pain was nowhere near as bad as it had been before.

"Hey! He's awake!" screamed the little boy. He jumped to his feet and raced out of the room.

Head spinning, Ron sat all the way up. He was on a grimy, torn mattress that was resting flat on the floor. A greasy-looking blanket covered his legs. The room had no windows, so he couldn't tell whether it was day or night.

There was a blurry mirror hanging crookedly on one wall. A corner of it was broken and a crack ran up its whole length. Ron couldn't tell if his face really looked as bad as it seemed, or if the mirror was making things worse than they really were. There was a huge shiner under his right eye and another big blue bruise along his left cheekbone. Holding up his left hand, he saw that it was still nearly black and swollen. But he could wiggle the fingers a little. Nothing broken.

He was drenched with sweat. The room was like an oven; no air moving at all.

Somebody came to the door that the boy had left open. Sylvia.

"You . . ." Ron began. Then he realized that he didn't know what he wanted to say.

She came over and knelt beside his mattress. "I was so scared you was gonna die."

"What happened? Where are we?"

She touched the bruise on his cheek, very lightly, just a fingertip. "Poor Ron . . . It was Dino. Him and some of his goons was waitin' fer you outside th' hotel."

It was almost funny. "And I was worried about you."

"About me?" She looked surprised.

"I was afraid he'd try to hurt you."

"Oh, Ron!" She put her arms around his shoulders. It hurt, he was still aching. But he held her there for a long moment.

Sylvia said into his ear, "I came back t' th' hotel to see if you was okay. I found you in th' lobby. I got you out just a coupla minutes before th' hardtops got there."

"Hardtops?"

"Helmet-heads. Cops." She pulled away from him. "Some tourist musta called 'em. If th' hardtops get you, they toss you in th' Tombs."

"But I'm a visitor. They can't do that."

"You got no money, no ID, nothin', right?"

"Oh . . . but still . . ."

"They woulda thought you were a gang kid. Or some weirdo got himself freaked out and beat up."

"Then—how do I get out? What day is it, anyway?"

"It's Monday, Labor Day. Th' gates close t'night at midnight and they won't open again 'till next summer. For tourists."

"I've got to get out!" Ron started to get up.

Sylvia put a hand on his shoulder. "Hold on, hold on. We'll getcha out. Al's gonna be here soon. Right? He'll figger out what t'do. You jest rest. Dino went over you pretty good."

Ron frowned. "How many of them were there?"

"I dunno," she said. "Four or five. Maybe six."

The little boy came back in. His eyes were wide with excitement. "Al's comin'! He's comin' up here *right now!*"

Then he raced out of the room again.

"Al knows what t'do," Sylvia said again.

For some reason that he didn't fully understand himself, Ron wanted to be on his feet when Al came in. He started to struggle up. Sylvia helped him.

The boy popped in again, his face red and sweaty. "He's here! Al's right here!"

Ron expected to see a tall, broad-shouldered, steel-eyed leader of men. Instead, the guy who stepped into the room was about his own age, short and wiry. He was much smaller and skinnier than Dino. There was a scar running across his chin and odd-looking wrinkles around his eyes.

"This is th' dude, huh?" Al's voice was soft, quiet.

Sylvia answered, "He's gotta be out before midnight or—"

"I know," Al said. "You an' th' kid split."

"But—"

"Split."

Sylvia gave Ron a worried glance. Then she tried to smile and said, "Good-bye, Ron."

"I'll see you later," Ron said as she went to the door.

Al looked Ron up and down. "Can you walk?"

"I think so."

"Okay. I'll give you directions t' th' nearest gate in th' Dome. It's about thirty blocks from here."

"Wait a minute," Ron said. "Before I go anywhere, I want my money back. And my ID and credit cards."

Al just stared at him.

"Well—you're supposed to know how to do things. How do I get this Dino guy? Do I have to call the police, or what?"

"The hardtops?" Al broke into a laugh. "The hardtops? Last time they was down here half of 'em never got out. They ain't been around here fer years."

"But Dino—"

"Forget it! Just be happy you're gettin' out. And alive."

"Now wait," Ron snapped, his temper rising. "Dino took more than a thousand dollars from me."

Al's face settled into a hard scowl. "Listen, punk. First off, nobody's gotta help you get out. I don't give a shit if you live or die, and nobody else does either, except that whacky Sylvia."

"What—"

"Second, whatever Dino took off ya is *his*. You want it back, you go find him and fight him for it. Only, this time he might not leave you breathin'. Catch?"

Ron felt his teeth clenching.

"An' third, Dino took yer cards and keys all right. But he didn't get any cash. Sylvia took that while you was sleepin'."

"*What?*"

"In th' hotel room," Al said.

"That's a damned lie!" Ron was suddenly shaking with fury.

"I got th' money off her," Al said, very calmly. "It belongs to us—"

"It's mine!"

"Not no more. It belongs to my gang. I'll help you get out— but only b'cause we got your money. Catch? Like you're buyin' your way outta th' Dome. You don't get nothin' fer free."

**R**on limped down an empty Manhattan street in the hot haze of late afternoon. He passed row after row of crumbling old buildings and empty store fronts. Windows blankly staring at him. No drapes or curtains or blinds. No glass left. No people. For all he could see, he was the only human being in Manhattan. The last man on Earth.

But inside those buildings there was life, Ron knew now. Rats scuttled in the darkness of the basements, and two-legged animals huddled in the rooms upstairs.

*She took my money.* Ron knew it was true. He didn't want to believe it, but he knew it was true. *She seemed so scared and alone, so soft and pretty . . . And it was all a trick. A lousy trick.*

Ron's feet hurt. Walking barefoot down streets covered with broken glass, old food cans, cigarette butts, torn paper, cracked cement that was steaming hot—he had cut one foot on something, and they were both coming up with blisters. His back and ribs still ached from the beating Dino and his friends had given him. His eyes were okay now, though the bruises still felt tender to the touch. His hand was still swollen painfully.

He couldn't get the thought of Sylvia out of his head. *She tricked me. She and Dino must have been working together*. But he kept remembering how it felt to hold her, the sweaty odor of her body, the words she whispered to him.

There were other people on the streets now. Visitors, all of them. Mostly middle-aged men. There were a few couples. Nobody Ron's age. They all were dressed well, but their clothes now looked rumpled, dirty. They were all heading in the same direction, toward the gate. They all looked tired.

A car drove by, a taxi honking at the pedestrians who were strolling in the street, pushing them out of its way. The taxi was filled with more visitors. A plume of sooty smoke trailed after it.

Ron felt completely bushed. He had been walking painfully for more than an hour. Finally, far up the street, he could see a thick crowd of people swarming. And beyond them, the heavy steel criss-cross beams of Manhattan Dome came down to street level.

The gate.

There were open shops and restaurants on the street now. People still buzzed in and out, doing their last bit of shopping or eating or drinking before the City closed down for the year. Everybody seemed to be rushing about even faster than usual. They looked wild-eyed, frenzied, like there were a million things they had to do before the gate closed.

But they didn't look happy at all. They didn't seem to be enjoying their fun.

*Is it really fun?* Ron wondered.

A pair of white-haired women came out of a shop gripping huge plastic bags that bulged with packages. They almost bumped into Ron because they were too busy talking to each other to notice him. He stepped back as they jostled past him. They stared at Ron as they passed.

"My goodness, look at him," said one to the other.

"Disgusting."

"Is that dirt or bruises?"

"What's the difference?" They headed toward the gate.

Ron stood there in the midst of the surging crowd. The people flowed around him the way water flows around an obstacle. They stared at his ragged clothes and bruised face. They talked about him. But no one spoke to him.

Above the heads of the crowd, Ron could see a policeman in his clean white helmet. For some reason he couldn't understand, Ron edged away from the gate, away from the policeman.

And then he saw Sylvia.

She was pushing through the thickening crowd, frowning and looking around. Searching for somebody.

*For me?* He was glad and angry and scared, all at the same time.

He made his way toward her. She spotted him and her eyes lit up. They both pushed through the crowd until they were standing face to face.

"I didn't know if I'd make it in time," she said, breathless.

She had to raise her voice to nearly a shout to be heard over the noise of the crowd.

"I don't have any more money," Ron heard himself say to her.

For a moment she didn't answer. The crowd pushed at them. It was hard to stay in place.

"Al toldja I took yer money. Right?"

"Right."

She shrugged and said nothing.

"Well, did you? Or was he lying?"

Sylvia shook her head. "No, he ain't a liar. I took it. While you was sleepin' in the hotel room."

Ron didn't know what to do, what to say. He stood there while the people streamed by, jostling them. The crowd was getting bigger and noisier. His head was hurting. Cars and buses full of people were honking and growling along the street. It was hot and dirty and noisy and confused.

"Why'd you come here?" he blurted.

"T' warn ya."

"Warn me?"

"About th' gate. They won't letcha through without an ID The hardtops'll throw ya in th' Tombs."

"What's the Tombs?"

Sylvia glanced across the crowd at the helmeted policeman. "It's like a big jail. Underground. It's real old and rotten. They toss ya in there, you never come out again. Nobody ever comes outta th' Tombs."

"They can't do that," Ron said.

"They sure can," she insisted, her eyes frightened. "I thought

Al gave you back yer ID But Dino's still got it. Gonna sell it fer fuel, he said. If you got no ID, the hardtops won't letcha outta th' Dome. They'll think yer one of us."

She was serious. "You really stay here in the City all year long?" Ron asked.

"Yeah. We can't get out."

"But . . . how come Al didn't warn me? Why would he just send me to the gate to be arrested? You told me—"

"Al don't care. He just wanted t' get rid of ya."

"And you *do* care?"

She frowned. "I . . . I don't wanna see nobody tossed in th' Tombs. Nobody. Ya never get out."

Ron thought a minute. "Then I've got to get my ID back from Dino."

"I can get it off him," Sylvia said.

"How?"

"I can do it, don't worry how."

He grabbed her by the shoulder. "How? The same way you got the money from me?"

Pulling away from his grip, Sylvia answered, "Yeah. Sort of."

Ron shook his head. "No. *I'll* get it back from Dino. I'll break him in half, if I have to. Come on."

He started pushing through the crowd back the way they had both come. Sylvia had to trot a few steps to catch up with him.

"You can't fight Dino . . . not like you are."

Ron said, "I can break every bone in his body with one hand."

"No . . . you can't . . ."

But Ron wouldn't listen. He kept walking. She stayed beside him, silent.

They walked up the street, away from the gate and the hectic crowd. They passed a hotel on the other side of the street. Men and women were leaning out of its windows, laughing and throwing things down onto the sidewalk. Somebody tossed a stuffed chair through a window, about ten flights up. It crashed through the glass and spun as it fell in a shower of glass shards. People on the sidewalk jumped and screamed as they raced out of the way. The chair hit the pavement like an explosion.

A woman collapsed and fell to the pavement. Others looked up, cursing and shaking their fists at the people in the windows. A sofa came tumbling down next, and everyone on the sidewalk scattered for safety.

A police car pulled up, its red roof light pulsing like a living heart. Four hardtops jumped out of the car and raced into the hotel.

"They must be crazy in there," Ron said.

"It's th' last night. They all go kinda flakey. Gonna be a tough night."

Ron shook his head. *And then they go home to be hard-working businessmen and loving fathers again. Until next summer.* Suddenly he started to wonder what his own father did every night while they visited the City together, every night when he left Ron in their hotel room watching TV while he went out and didn't return until Ron was sound asleep.

Smoke was coming from one of the hotel windows now. A

woman was screaming, and Ron could hear the deeper shouts of angry men.

"They're all sick," Sylvia said.

They walked on. Ron forgot how tired he was, because his stomach was reminding him about how many meals he had missed. He was *hungry*. He'd never felt really hungry before in his life. It hurt.

Police cars cruised through the streets, but soon the crowd thinned down and Ron and Sylvia were in a part of the City that was deserted. They walked alone up the empty, filthy, littered sidewalks. He didn't speak to her. He couldn't. Sylvia remained silent, too, until: "You think I'm a crud, dontcha?"

"Should I be happy that you stole my money?"

"I . . ." Sylvia looked confused. "I don't know how to say it right, Ron. Like . . . I don't wantcha t' think I'm a crud."

He kept walking.

It was hard for her to keep up with him. She nearly had to run. "Okay, I clipped yer money. Right? But . . . that had nothin' t' do with whether I like ya or not. Catch? Th' money's just money. It ain't you and me."

"It was my money. And I trusted you."

"Yeah, but me and Al and the kids need it more'n you. You can get more. We can't. Not 'til next summer."

"And you needed it so much you had to steal it."

"I needed it fer Davey an' me. He's jest a little kid . . . he hasta have food all winter."

"Couldn't you get a job?"

She looked at Ron as if he were crazy. "A job? How'm I

gonna get a job? All th' jobs're taken by people who live outside th' City. They come in fer two months in th' summer and make enough t' live on th' rest a th' year."

"Well, you could apply for a job too," Ron insisted. "There are employment centers where they can find jobs for you."

Sylvia stopped walking. "Ron, you jest don't unnerstand. We got no ID's. None of th' kids. We don't exist! As far as th' hardtops an' th' computers an' th' world outside th' Dome's concerned, *we don't exist*. They throw us in th' Tombs an' get rid of us whenever they catch one of us."

Ron felt his face squeezing into a frown, as if that would help his brain to understand what she was telling him. "You mean you really live here inside the Dome all year long . . . and the government doesn't take care of you at all?"

"That's right. Al, Dino, all th' gangs. Lotsa people. Some grown-ups, too. We all live here all year long."

"But that's against the law! The Dome's closed for most of the year. New York was evacuated years ago—"

"The law!" Sylvia laughed. "Th' hardtops leave at midnight. From then on 'til next July, there ain't no law inside th' Dome. Al's th' boss in our turf. Every gang's got its own leader and its own turf."

It was finally starting to sink into Ron's brain. "And you live here all the time. In that—that rat hole I was in?"

Nodding, Sylvia answered, "Right. That's home fer Davey an' me an' all Al's gang. That's why I needed yer money. T' get us through th' winter. Gotta buy food and everything."

Horrified, Ron said, "But you *can't* live there all the time. Not in there! Not like that!"

"We all do," she said simply.

Without even thinking about it, Ron said, "Well, you're not going to anymore." He started walking again. Faster than ever.

"Whaddaya mean?" Sylvia hurried alongside him.

"I'm getting you out of here. Tonight. You can't live here. I won't let you."

"But I *can't* get out, Ron. I can't!"

"Why not?"

She looked scared. "Ya need an ID card. I never had one. I was born here. They'll never let me through th' gates. They'll put me in th' Tombs!"

"No they won't," Ron said firmly. "I'll get my ID from Dino. I'll tell the police that you're with me and your ID was stolen. I'll get you through."

"No. I can't."

"Why not?"

"Davey," she said.

"The little kid?"

Nodding, Sylvia said, "I'm the only one he's got t' take care of him. I can't leave him all by himself."

Ron glanced at his wrist, forgetting that Dino had taken his watch. "Come on, time's getting short. We'll take Davey with us."

"You'll what?"

"We'll take Davey too. Come on."

She kept pace beside him. "You really wanna do this?"

"Yes."

"And Davey too?"

"I'm not going to let you rot here."

"But we was born here. We make out all right."

Ron just shook his head. Sylvia looked at him in a funny way. But she stayed beside him.

The building she lived in was even filthier and more crumbled-down than Ron had remembered it. It had apparently been a factory building once, part of a long row of such buildings jammed side-by-side the length of the long city block. Most of the other buildings were ten stories high; hers was twelve stories. Across the narrow street, an empty garage yawned at them, the sidewalk in front of it stained and slick with ancient grease spills.

At the street level, the building had once had big store windows. Now they were boarded up with old, warped boards that were covered with the remains of a thousand posters and ragged, hand-scrawled graffiti that Ron couldn't understand. A handful of dark-looking boys were sitting on the low step in front of the building's main doorway as they came up. One of the boys said something to Sylvia in a foreign language. Ron had taken Spanish in school, and this sounded vaguely like it, but he couldn't make it out. Sylvia clacked out a few fast words in the same dialect and the boys laughed.

"What did he say?" Ron asked as they stepped through the doorway.

"Nothin'."

They walked quickly up four flights of creaking wooden stairs to Sylvia's room. The building was like an oven, hot and breathless. Ron was bathed in sweat by the time they got to the fourth floor. Her room was bare. The only things in it were a battered old chest, like a wooden box, sitting in one corner, and a mattress next to it, half covered by a dirty bedspread. The walls were grimy and cracked, with gaps in the plaster. A few posters and pictures torn from old magazines tried to cover up the worst spots on the walls. It was like putting a few band-aids on a man who had fallen off a cliff.

Ron stayed by the hallway door as Sylvia walked through the bare little room and into the room beyond.

"Davey's not here," she said. "Wait a minute 'til I find him. You want somethin' t' drink?"

Ron nodded. His mouth was desert-dry. He wanted to ask if there was anything to eat, but decided not to.

Sylvia led him into the "kitchen," an even tinier room, blazing hot, without any windows at all. There was a shelf built into one wall and a shaky-looking chair next to it. On one side of the shelf sat a stubby little refrigerator.

Sylvia opened the refrigerator and pulled out a plastic bottle of juice. "Here, have some of this while I find Davey."

She handed Ron the bottle. It was warm. The refrigerator wasn't working. He looked around for a glass. There were none. The only thing on the shelf next to him was a dead insect, reddish and ugly-looking, curled on its back with its thin legs poking stiffly upward.

"I'll be right back. He's prob'ly downstairs, playin' with some of the other kids."

She left. Ron sat on the chair. It groaned as his weight settled on it. The juice bottle felt sticky. He got up and opened the refrigerator. There was nothing else in it.

The heat was awful. Ron felt sweat trickling down his face, his neck, his ribs, arms, and legs. He looked around again for a glass, a plastic cup, anything. No chance. Finally he rubbed the lip of the juice bottle with the torn edge of his not-very-clean sleeve. Then he took a long swallow of the juice.

It tasted funny. Different. But wet and good.

He took another drink, then walked out into the bigger room, still holding the bottle in his hand. Maybe there was a window he could open. His head was buzzing and his eyes were starting to feel very heavy.

*The heat*, he thought.

Ron stood in the middle of the room and stared at the posters on the walls. They were moving! Shimmering, the way water sparkles when sunshine strikes it. Ron blinked at the posters and tried to shake his head. For the first time since Dino's guys had beaten him, his body felt fine—no pain at all, everything loose and warm and good. He was floating, weightless and happy. He heard himself laughing. The posters were floating now, too. Swirling around his head, colors shifting and glowing and everything going around and around and around . . .

**W**hen Ron opened his eyes again he was sprawled face down on the grimy mattress. Some sort of red-brown bug was crawling an inch past his nose.

He jerked away from the insect and bumped into Sylvia, who was sitting next to him.

"You okay?" She looked guilty.

It took a long moment for Ron to get everything together in his head. "There was something in the drink . . . you stoned me!"

"I had to, Ron. Honest . . . you was gonna drag me out t' th' gate . . . you woulda just got us both tossed in th' Tombs."

"But I was going to take you back to my home."

"They wouldn't let us through th' gate. Al was jest tryin' t' get rid of you. I thought he was gonna help ya. When I found out what he did I came after you . . ."

For the first time, Ron saw that there was daylight filtering through the dirt-caked window.

"What time is it?" he shrieked.

"Morning. Tuesday morning. All th' gates're closed."

Ron scrambled to his feet. "No, it can't be! I've got to get out of here."

"You can't," Sylvia said flatly. She got up and stood beside Ron. "Nobody gets out now. Not 'til next summer."

He grabbed her by the shoulders. Hard. "You did this to me! First you robbed me and now you've locked me up in here!"

She wasn't scared. And if his grip hurt her, she didn't let him see it.

"I ain't gonna let nobody get me put in th' Tombs," Sylvia said. "I like you, Ron. I toldja that before, right? But you was jest gonna get both of us into th' Tombs. Them hardtops down at th' gates don't listen to nobody that ain't got an ID."

He let her go and turned to stare at the window. "I've got to get out of here," he muttered.

"Not now," Sylvia said. "Not 'til next summer. And you gotta get yer ID off Dino before he sells it."

Ron looked sharply at her.

"I gotta get Davey," Sylvia said.

She left him alone in the grimy, crumbling room. Ron walked slowly to the window. There was nothing to see through its gray-filmed panes except the cracked, stained back wall of another brick building.

His mind was spinning. *I can't stay here for a year! There must be some way out. Dad will get the police to come in and look for me. Got the National Exams . . . got to make my Career vector choice . . .*

He turned and looked toward the open door. *Sylvia! It's all her fault.* But his mind kept picturing her face, her body, how it felt to hold her, how much he wanted to be holding her right now. *She saved my life. And if the Tombs are as bad as she says they are . . .*

Then a different thought came to him. He tried to picture what his mother and father would do if he brought Sylvia home. Ron couldn't imagine what they'd do. Except that he knew they wouldn't let her stay. They'd turn her over to the police. *That's just what they'd do. Maybe she really is better off here.*

But he shook his head. *Here?* Looking around the littered, filthy, bare, bug-infested room, Ron could hardly believe it. *The jails back home are better than this.*

Sylvia came back at last, pulling Davey along with one hand and carrying a bag of food in the other. They sat on the floor together, the three of them, while she handed out rolls and cheese and plastic cups of something that was supposed to be coffee. It was warm, not hot, and it tasted like machine oil.

"Where did you get this?" Ron asked.

Sylvia munched on a bite of roll and answered thickly, "Downstairs. First floor. Al's got a big stack of food an' stuff. Leftovers from th' tourists."

*Stolen*, Ron knew. But it was the best meal he'd ever had.

He wolfed down the food greedily, thinking about beggars and choosers.

"We gotta get Al t' let you in th' gang," Sylvia said. "Otherwise yer gonna be in tough shape."

"The gang?"

"Al's gang. He's th' boss. He's out someplace on th' turf right now. Be back t'night."

"And what do I do all day?"

"Stay here. Dino's around, an' if he knows yer here he'll start in on you again. He likes t' lean on people."

"Dino hits hard," Davey said, in his high little voice. "He hits me when I'm bad."

Ron stared at the child, then looked up at Sylvia. "He hits Davey?"

She nodded, her face grim. "That's why I want th' two of you t' stay right here all day. No trouble if you stay here."

"And what about you?"

"I'll be around. Hafta go out this afternoon fer a while, get some food. Wish that damned 'frigerator worked. I could put food in there instead a goin' out twice a day."

Ron said, "Maybe I can fix it. Are there any tools around?"

Davey scrambled to his feet. "I know! There's big tools inna basement, next t' th' furnace. Eddie and me seen 'em when we was playin' down there!"

"Let's take a look at them." Ron started to get up.

Sylvia stopped him with a hand on his shoulder. "No—you stay right here. Davey, you go down an' get all th' tools you can carry. Bring 'em up here. But don't tell nobody Ron's up here. Unnerstand?"

Davey nodded eagerly. His big dark eyes went from Sylvia to

Ron. "Okay. I be quiet." He looked very serious and excited at the same time.

So Ron spent the morning taking the refrigerator apart. It kept his mind busy, kept him from thinking about what was happening back home, thinking about his father, his mother, the Examiner. He just worked on the refrigerator and tried to keep his mind blank.

Davey squatted on the kitchen floor next to him, hardly saying a word, watching intently. He took in every move that Ron made, until Ron felt that the child could have copied everything he did, move for move.

Sylvia left in the afternoon. By then, Ron had figured out what was wrong with the refrigerator. It was simply dirt. The motor was very old, but still good. It was just clogged with dust and greasy grime. Davey found some plastic sheets that were almost as dirty as the motor itself, and they used the sheets to clean the motor, piece by piece. Davey helped, although Ron had to re-do almost every piece the boy worked on.

By mid-afternoon the refrigerator was humming smoothly and getting cold.

"We did it!" Davey shouted.

Ron grinned and rubbed a hand through the boy's curly black hair.

The afternoon heat was getting fierce. The little kitchen was like a furnace. Ron went into the other room, and for the first time he saw that there was an air-conditioner set into a niche below the window.

"Hey Davey, bring those tools in here."

It was dark by the time they finished. The air-conditioner's main problem was also dirt. But there was also a bad coil in the motor and a couple of loose connections. Ron and Davey sneaked up to an empty room on the next floor and stole pieces from the air-conditioner there.

"Now don't tell Sylvia we left the apartment," Ron said to Davey. "She'll get upset."

Davey grinned a huge grin. "Okay Ron. It's a secret. Right?"

Ron nearly got sick when he saw Davey's grin. The boy's teeth were almost all rotted black stumps.

By the time Sylvia came back the rooms were cooled off, and Ron's stomach was growling with hunger. She looked surprised as she came through the doorway, carrying a plastic bag in one arm.

"It's cool in here!" she said, delighted. "Howdja do it?"

Davey bounded up to her. "We fixed th' 'frigimader and we fixed the air commissioner. Ron an' me!"

"Wow," Sylvia said. She handed Davey the plastic bag, it was small and light enough for him to carry. She went over to the air-conditioner and stood in front of it.

"This's great. It's hotter'n hell out on th' streets."

Ron smiled. "Wasn't much."

"It's terrific." Sylvia came over and kissed him lightly. "C'mon, let's eat. Al's comin' up here later on."

Dinner was nothing more than a few pieces of cold meat and a single bottle of beer. Davey drank the beer, too. There was nothing else.

But Sylvia was planning ahead. "With th' 'frigerator fixed I can stock some food an' keep milk fer Davey. An'—hey, Ron, can you fix cookers? There's a cooker sittin' in an empty kitchen upstairs. If we can get it down here an' get it goin' . . . wow, it'll be great! Right?"

He laughed. "Right."

Davey went to sleep right there on the floor. Sylvia picked him up and brought him to the mattress and laid him down gently. Then she pulled the bedcover up over him. Both the mattress and the cover were so filthy that Ron shuddered.

"He's a bright kid," Ron said quietly.

Sylvia nodded.

There was a knock at the door, and it swung open before they could move to answer it. Al came into the room, his face dark as a thundercloud.

"So yer back," he said.

Before Ron could answer, Sylvia said, "I brought him back. You was jest gonna let th' hardtops flip him."

For a moment, Al stood there at the door and said nothing. He glanced at Davey curled up on the mattress, then quietly shut the door behind him.

"Okay. Let's sit down and talk." They squatted on the floor like three Indians.

For the first time, Ron saw that Al was tired. There was tension in his face. His eyes were blood-shot. Tight lines were etched around his mouth and eyes.

"Now lissen," Al said. "We can't feed no extra mouths all winter. That's why I hadda get ridda ya. It's tough enough gettin' food fer all the mouths we got already without puttin' on a dude from Outside. Catch?"

Ron realized that Al was trying to be honest. Maybe even fair. "What do I do, then?" he asked.

Al shrugged. "All I know is, we can't feed no extra mouths."

Slyvia broke in, "But Ron can help th' gang! He can fix machines an' stuff. Look, he fixed the air-conditioner. An' th' 'frigerator in th' kitchen. He can fix anything. Right, Ron?"

"Well, not anything—"

She went on, "I bet he can fix th' whatsit down in th' basement that always blows out."

"The generator," Al said.

"You have a generator downstairs?" Ron asked. "So that's where the electricity comes from."

"It's always conkin' out," Al admitted. "We hafta pay a guy from another gang t' fix it, or else we go without power. Costs plenty, too."

Ron nodded.

"Can you fix it?" Al asked flatly.

"I won't know until I see it," Ron answered. "But I've fixed generators before, and motors, and lots of other stuff."

"Gun?" Al asked suddenly. "Can you fix guns?"

Ron shrugged. "I don't know. I never tried. But if they're not too complicated . . ."

Al eyed him suspiciously. "Okay. We'll see. Come on down to th' basement an' take a look at th' generator."

They started to get up. But Sylvia stopped them for a moment. "Al, what happens if Ron can't fix th' generator?"

"Then he's out. He either knows how t' fix things or he don't. If he can fix machines, then he can help us, an' we keep him. If he can't, then he goes out onna street."

"On his own?"

"Yeah."

"But he'll die. They'll kill him. Nobody can live on th' streets by himself."

"I know," Al said. He wasn't being cruel. It was simply a flat statement of truth.

It was an old, old generator, powered by an even older diesel engine that roared and clattered and spewed a fine mist of oil spray through the musty air of the basement. A dim light hung over the machinery. In the shadows Ron could make out a half-dozen drums of diesel fuel.

"How on earth do you get diesel fuel here?" he wondered aloud.

"Never mind," Al said. "We get it. That's all you gotta know."

Ron shrugged and went up close to the machinery. The oil spray stung his eyes. He shouted over the noise, "How long does it run between breakdowns?"

Al waved a hand. "Coupla weeks. Sometimes more, sometimes less."

Ron could see that the generator was held together with little more than bubble gum and prayer. It vibrated dangerously. In time it would shake itself apart.

He stepped back to where Al and Sylvia stood.

"Can you get spare parts?"

Al said, "You show us whatcha need an' we'll get it for you."

"Okay."

"Can ya fix it?" Al shouted.

"Sure. Had one just like it in school, in mechanical repair class. Our auxiliary generator at home is a later model—"

"Okay, okay. You can stay 'til it stops runnin' again. If you can fix it, great. If you can't . . ." He jerked his thumb in an old baseball umpire's gesture that meant *out*.

Ron said, "We ought to shut it down and overhaul it, put in new parts, get it back in good shape. Then it won't break down on you."

"Shut it off on purpose?"

"Yes."

Al shook his head. "Naw, I don't like that. It stops all by itself often enough. I ain't gonna shut it down on purpose."

"But—"

Al walked away from him.

They went back upstairs. Ron could still hear the clattering of the diesel engine. His ears were ringing from the noise. His skin felt slimy with machine oil.

"Okay," Al said when they reached the ground floor. "You stay until it quits workin' again. Now go find a room of yer own. I don't wantcha stayin' with my girl no more."

Ron felt the air gasp out of him, as if someone had punched him in the gut. *Your girl?* he asked silently. He looked at Sylvia, but she wouldn't look back at him.

"An' come see me first thing t'morrow mornin'," Al commanded. "We'll start gettin' those parts you want."

Ron nodded dumbly.

He turned and headed for the stairs. *His girl. Sylvia's his girl? Then why did she . . .* All at once it hit him. *She's agreed to be his girl to save me!*

Ron didn't sleep that night. Not at all.

He saw daylight come, slowly brightening the window of the room he had picked. With the Dome over Manhattan, you never got any direct sunlight, just a gradual brightness that had to fight its way through the dirt-streaked windows.

Ron had picked out a room on the floor above Sylvia's. It was blazing hot, but he knew he could get the air-conditioner working soon enough.

Now he lay sprawled on a mattress, hands under his head, watching the daylight come to the city. And wondering about Sylvia. Wondering and worrying.

He heard the door to the hallway creak open.

"Ron?" It was Davey's high thin voice.

Sitting up, Ron answered, "Right here, Davey."

The boy ran in and knelt beside him. "Hi, Ron. Al says we're gonna go out on a raid t'day! An' you're comin'!"

"A raid?"

Davey nodded. He was almost trembling, he was so excited. "Th' warriors're meetin' up on th' roof. Al says fer you t' come up right away."

Puzzled, frowning, Ron followed Davey up flights of creaking steps to the roof. More than two dozen guys were already there, clustered around Al.

The roof was the highest of all the buildings in the block. Ron could look out over the rooftops of the nearby buildings and see the gray ribwork of the Dome, dim and misty in the distance. The roof was covered with black gravel-like stuff that crunched and stung under Ron's bare feet. There was something wrong about the place, though. It took Ron a few moments to realize what it was: no wind. If he had been this high back home at the Tracts, on a building roof or a hill, there would have been a breeze. But here under the Dome there wasn't any. At least, not at that particular moment.

"Here he is now," Al said as Ron stood uncertainly near the door at the top of the stairs.

All the guys turned to look at him.

"Come over here," Al said, waving to Ron. "This's Ron," he told the others as Ron walked gingerly over the rough gravel to him. "He's from Outside an' he knows howta fix machines. We're goin' over t' Chelsea turf t' get some parts he needs t' fix th' generator downstairs."

"It ain't broke." Ron saw that it was Dino who spoke.

Dino grinned at Ron. He was wearing Ron's boots. *And he's got my ID card, too*, Ron said to himself. He took a step toward Dino.

But Al grabbed his arm. "Now lissen!" he snapped. "I'm tel-lin' both of ya. There ain't no room for bad blood in this gang. You guys got a beef—bury it! Unnerstand? No fightin' between gang members. We got a raid t' pull off. You wanna fight, then fight the Chelsea warriors. They ain't gonna let us come in and take what we want, just for the askin'."

So Ron stood there glaring while Dino grinned back at him. Al started to tell of his plan for the raid, pointing toward some distant rooftops to show what he meant to do.

"They won't be expectin' a raid so soon after the gates closed down," one of the guys said.

"Right," Al answered. "Now, Dino'll lead th' main force right down th' middle o' their turf"—he pointed toward a group of high, blocky looking buildings—"an' make 'em think we're goin' for their headquarters."

"They'll think we're tryin' t' grab their broads!"

"Them pigs. Erg!"

Everybody laughed.

"Okay, okay," Al said, quieting them down. "Now, while Dino an' th' main force're makin' a big fight in th' center of their turf, me an' Ron and a few other guys swing 'round to the warehouses"—Al pointed to another row of gray, worn-looking buildings—"an' grab th' stuff Ron needs. We gotta do it quick, before th' Chelsea guys find out what we're up to."

As Al went on talking, Ron began to realize what was going to happen. This was going to be a raid. A real fight. Like Indians raiding a town in the old West. Like knights storming a castle. The gang was a little army. They were going to fight another gang, another army. They would kill people.

He saw that most of the guys had weapons on them. Dino had a pistol stuck in his belt. Others had pistols, rifles, knives, chains, clubs, and strange-looking things that Ron couldn't figure out.

And out of the corner of his eye, Ron noticed Davey and three other little boys. They were crouched near the door to the stairs, listening to every word, big-eyed with excitement. They watched the older guys, stared at their weapons. *They can't wait until they're old enough to be warriors,* Ron realized. *Old enough to get killed.*

"Okay, let's go," Al said.

Everybody started to move toward the door and down the stairs. Ron stood still and let the other guys flow past him.

Dino came up to him, still grinning. "Whatsamatter, dude? You look scared."

Al stepped between them. "Knock it off, Dino. Get movin'. You're supposed t' be leadin' th' main force, not makin' chatter."

"Go hump yourself," Dino muttered. But he turned away and headed for the stairs.

Al shook his head. "He's gettin' too lousy for his own good. Gonna hafta stop him one of these days."

Ron said nothing.

"Okay, kid," Al said. "You come with me."

Ron hesitated for just a bare second. Then he followed Al to the stairs. *No use arguing,* he told himself. *You either go with them or they throw you to the wolves. You're either part of the gang or you're dead.*

Still, Ron knew that there was going to be fighting—killing—because of him.

Al led him down into the street and around the corner. A battered old Army truck was sitting at curbside, waiting for them.

Al went around to the tailgate and swung himself up. Then he reached a hand out and helped Ron up into the truck. There were eight other guys already in the truck, sitting on the floor. The plastic roof and sides made it dark and cool inside. Al sat down nearest the open tailgate. Ron sat next to him.

"One other thing we got goin' for us," Al said as the truck started up with a roar and a rattle, "is we got gas to run with. Stashed a lot of it all summer long. Better'n goin' in on foot."

Shaking and lurching, the truck groaned away from the curb and started down the street. Ron couldn't see much out of the open tailgate. Just empty streets. Totally empty. Nobody on the sidewalks at all. No other cars driving by. Not even any cars parked at the curbs. The city was really empty.

Except for the gangs.

After many blocks, the truck stopped. But the driver kept the engine running. Ron felt its low, fast vibration in his bones. He tried to figure out where they were. There was a strange smell in the air; a foul smell, like the stink bomb one of his friends had made once in chemistry class.

Al sniffed it too. "Humpin' sewers backin' up already," he muttered.

"Soon's they close down th' garbage plants," said one of the guys deeper in the truck.

"Them Chelsea clowns must like th' smell," somebody said.

"They think it's perfoom!"

They laughed.

"Keep it quiet," Al snapped. "Lissen for th' signal."

They stilled down. For several minutes there was nothing to

hear except the ticking of the truck's engine. Ron mentally diagnosed a sticky valve. The engine would need an overhaul soon, or at least a tune-up.

An explosion! The sudden blasting noise made Ron jump.

"That's it!" Al shouted. "Let's *go!*"

The driver heard him and put the truck in gear, with a horrible grinding noise. The truck lurched forward, engine roaring. Down the streets they raced, buildings whizzing by, windows blank and staring.

Al stood up. Bracing himself and holding tight to the metal framework that supported the plastic roof, he leaned out and looked around the end of the truck to see where they were. The wind tore at his curly hair and made him squint.

He pulled himself back inside and hunched down again. "Hang on tight!" he yelled.

Everybody pulled his knees up to his chest and grabbed his ankles. Ron did the same.

The truck hit something with an ear-splitting crash and a jar that rattled Ron's teeth. Then they drove inside a huge building, the truck's engine suddenly sounding hollow and even noisier than before.

They stopped with a lurch that slid everybody into a jumbled heap. Al jumped out of the truck before the last echo of the engine's roar had died away.

"C'mon, c'mon, let's go!" he yelled.

Ron jumped down to the floor of the warehouse and the other guys piled out behind him. They all had guns in their hands. Two guys had automatic rifles, the rest had pistols.

The eight armed men sprinted to the doors that the truck had just crashed through. Ron looked around and saw row after row of packing crates, stacked up as high as the ceiling, which must have been at least six stories up.

"Okay," Al snapped. "Find whatcha need and let's get it packed in th' truck. Quick! We ain't got all day."

"I can't go running through a strange warehouse and pick out everything we need in a few minutes," Ron complained. "This is no way to—"

Al cut him short. "This's the *only* way yer gonna get whatcha need. Now get busy and stop yappin'!"

With a shrug, Ron turned toward the stacks of equipment. Al and the truck driver and another guy, who must have been up in the cab with the driver, went with Ron.

At least the crates were clearly marked with stenciled lettering. And further back there were smaller pieces of equipment wrapped in clear plastic, so Ron could see what they were.

He spent nearly an hour pacing up and down the rows of equipment, picking out as much as he could find. The driver and his helper carried most of the stuff back to the truck. Al stayed with Ron. He had a gun tucked into his waistband. *Is he protecting me or making sure I won't try to run away?* Ron wondered.

"Time's gettin' short," Al muttered.

"Okay. I think I've got most of what I need," Ron said.

A shot echoed through the warehouse.

"They found us!" somebody shouted.

"C'mon, let's go," Al said.

He and Ron started sprinting back to the truck. The driver and his helper were already there, loading some of the equipment Ron had picked out.

But as they ran, Ron's eye caught a glimpse of the lettering on one of the big crates: CHARLESTON TURBOGENERATOR MARK VIII.

Ron skidded to a halt. "Wow! Can we get that into the truck?"

Al had to scuttle back a dozen steps. "It's big—"

"And it's heavy," Ron said. "We'll need at least six guys to carry it. But it'll be worth it."

Al glanced over his shoulder toward the truck and the smashed front gate where his eight fighters were crouched tensely, waiting for an enemy attack. Then he looked back at the big plastic crate.

"Dimmy, Lou, Patsy, Ed—come over here, quick!"

Al got the driver to back the truck up to the end of the row where the generators were stacked. Then the six of them heaved and lifted and strained to get one of the big crates onto the back of the truck. Ron and Al helped, too. Ron felt its weight against his shoulders, felt sweat breaking out on him as they struggled to get the crate high enough to slide into the truck. He wished for a powered forklift.

More shots! Guys shouting, cursing. Somebody screamed with pain.

They got the crate into the truck. Ron's arms seemed to float away from him once the load of the turbogenerator was taken away.

They scrambled up into the truck. The driver edged it out toward the gate and the other warriors who had been defending the gate against the Chelsea fighters clambered in. One of them was badly hurt. He had to be pulled in. His face and chest were covered with blood, and he moaned sickeningly.

Ron stared at him as they dumped him on the floor of the truck, next to the generator crate. The truck roared out into the daylight, and into a hail of enemy fire. Bullets whizzed by and clanged off metal. The guys flattened themselves on the truck floor. All except Al, who knelt at the tailgate and fired back with an automatic rifle. The shattering noise of the gun's blasting shut everything else off from Ron's brain.

Only when the gun stopped firing could Ron open his tight-squeezed eyes. He smelled sharp, bitter, slightly oily fumes from the gun. He felt the wind ripping through the truck from a hundred bullet holes in the plastic sides.

Then he saw that he was lying next to the wounded boy. Ron backed away, his hands and knees sliding on the blood-slippery truck floor. Ron found that his clothes, his hands, even his face were sticky with the kid's blood.

"How's he?" Al asked.

"Dead," somebody answered.

And then Ron was leaning out of the truck, over the tailgate, vomiting. He could feel his stomach twisting inside him. All the strength left him.

*Is that what it's like here? Is this the way I'm going to have to live?*

**S**o Ron became a member of Al's gang. Its formal name was the Gramercy Association, Ron found out, although no one ever told him why it was called that, or where the name came from. No one seemed to know. To each of the hundred or so members, it was simply Al's gang. Al was their leader, tough, wary, totally without a smile in him, but as fair as any leader of a pack of wild teenagers could be.

It took several weeks before they made Ron a real member of the gang. But when the generator down in the basement of their building conked out and Ron had it fixed and running again in a few hours, Al reached out his hand and shook with Ron. That night the gang's inner council met up on the roof and voted Ron in as a full gang member. Only Dino voted against him.

In the following weeks, Ron tried to get a firmer idea of where they were and just how large the gang actually was. He spent much of his time repairing things, from air-conditioners to rusted-out revolvers. In the evenings, though, he'd walk around the deserted streets and gawk at the high, empty buildings. Most of them had been lofts or factories. A few were once apartment buildings. One of the smallest in the area had a tiny plaque on it that Ron could barely make out through the grime and rust that had accumulated.

BIRTHPLACE OF
THEODORE ROOSEVELT
TWENTY-SIXTH PRESIDENT
OF THE
UNITED STATES

Every window in the four-story building was broken. Its stone front was blackened by fire.

There were at least a hundred members of the gang, two-thirds of them male, teen-aged or in their early twenties. The number seemed to shift every day. On raids, Al would never take fewer than twenty warriors, usually more like thirty or forty. He always left a fair-sized group of fighters back at their home turf to defend their headquarters and the women and children.

After that first raid, Ron stayed strictly inside Gramercy turf. Al announced that Ron was a mechanic, not a warrior. He was too valuable to risk in fighting. Al had Ron repairing everything the gang owned, from generators to guns. Especially guns.

For there were raids every week. Raids on other gangs. Counterraids by neighboring gangs into the Gramercy turf. Ron nearly got caught in one of them, one evening as he was walking alone on the streets. He had to hide in a deserted basement until the shooting was over. It was scary, because the basement wasn't totally deserted, after all: it was alive with rats.

There were raids to gain revenge for something that had happened the previous winter. Raids to get even for someone else's revenge raid. Dino took a small group of warriors out one night and brought back a half-dozen girls, none of them older than fifteen, who immediately were voted into membership in the Gramercy gang. They didn't seem to mind much.

One afternoon Ron was sitting in his room, tinkering with an automatic rifle. His room looked more like a workshop than a living place. And it was. Tools were stacked everywhere, in shelves that Ron had made himself. Not quite by himself: little Davey had become Ron's helper and almost constant companion. The only place in the room where there were no tools or pieces of equipment waiting to be fixed was Ron's bed, an old cot that Davey had found down in the basement.

Ron frowned as he disassembled the firing mechanism of the rifle. He didn't like guns and didn't like working on them. But Al gave the orders, and if Ron wanted to eat, he fixed the guns.

Sylvia walked in and stopped a few paces from the door. Even though the room was air-conditioned, she left the door open. She was wearing a sleeveless jumper and microskirt that had once been white, but would never be white again.

Ron forced himself to stay in his chair behind the work table. "Hello," he said, keeping his voice calm.

"Hi. You seen Davey?"

"He's outside playing. I told him he shouldn't spend all day cooped up in here."

"Oh. Yeah, I guess that's good . . . Howya doin'?"

"Fine," Ron said.

"Ever'body says yer great at fixin' things."

He nodded.

She wouldn't come any closer. "Uh . . . you been eatin' okay?"

"Sure." It was a lie. Ron had been hungry from his first day with the gang. But no hungrier than anyone else. The kids just didn't have much food. They had piled up some canned and other packaged foods during the summer, when most of the gang members had either found jobs among the tourist centers or stolen food. Some of their raids on other gangs had been for the purpose of "liberating" food supplies. And there was some sort of a market uptown somewhere, Ron had heard, a black market that somehow brought in fresh food from outside the Dome and sold it for enormous prices. Al wouldn't let any of the gang members deal with the black market, however. Too expensive, he insisted. And they all obeyed him, despite their constant grumbling hunger.

"Ever'body been treatin' you okay?" Sylvia asked. "Dino or nobody givin' you trouble, are they?"

Ron put the rifle mechanism down. There was no sense trying to work while she was in the room.

"No. No trouble from anybody."

"Good," Sylvia said.

She was so pretty! For a long moment neither of them said anything.

Then finally Sylvia asked, "You wanna come down t' my place for dinner? Got some special frozen stuff Al took offa the East River guys yesterday."

Ron's stomach trembled with anticipation. But he said, "No thanks. You and Al enjoy it."

"Al's out," she said. "He's talkin' t' some other gang chiefs, tryin' t' set up a truce or somethin'. Too many raids, ever'body's hurtin'."

"When will he be back?" Ron heard himself ask.

Sylvia shrugged.

Shaking his head, Ron said, "Look, you're his girl now, and I . . ."

"So what? I still like you."

"Yes, but—well, where I come from, you stay with one guy. It could just cause trouble."

Sylvia almost laughed at him. "Cheez, you must come from a real bughouse. Is everybody up-tight on the Outside like you?"

"Look, Sylvia, I appreciate what you've done for me. You saved my life and, well . . . is Al treating you all right?"

"Sure. Why shouldn't he?"

"You like being his girl?"

"Sure."

"Sure," Ron echoed.

It took a minute for Sylvia to understand what Ron meant. "Hey, I dunno what's goin' on inside yer head, Ron. But get one thing down. I *always* been Al's girl. Right? Ever since he was chief of th' gang. Even before that, I was his girl. Catch?"

Ron felt as if a truck had hit him. "But . . . but . . . you and me . . ."

"I like you an awful lot, Ron. Some ways, yer nicer'n Al. Yer awful sweet. But I'm Al's girl. Nuthin' we can do about that."

"Then—what you just said . . ."

She shrugged. "But I'm still his girl."

Al was gone for three days, and all during that time Ron stayed in his own room. Davey brought him some food, but most of the time Ron stayed hungry. And sleepless. He stared into the darkness each night, thinking of Sylvia and hating himself twice over. Once for thinking of her, and again for not doing anything about it.

When Al finally got back, he was glowing with happiness. He called a council meeting up on the roof. Ron was included in the meeting.

Al paced up and down along the crunching gravel as he talked. The other guys stood or squatted on their heels. Ron stayed on the fringes of the twelve-man council, on his feet.

"Musta been twenty-five, thirty gang chiefs there," Al said excitedly, waving his hands eagerly as he spoke. "We met in the Empire State buildin', down on th' ground floor. Y'know they's a dozen gangs livin' right inside the building? On different floors. One of 'em never comes down t' th' street at all! Grows its own food up on th' roofs. Creepy."

Ron looked at the council members. They didn't seem very impressed. None of them could think as fast or as far as Al, Ron realized. That's what had made Al the gang's leader. He could plan ahead, he could see farther than any of the others. He wasn't the best fighter among the bunch, but he could get the fighters to work together and do better as a team than they could ever hope to do as individuals.

"Why'n't we take over th' whole Empire State buildin'?" Dino asked, grinning. "Make some headquarters, huh?"

Al threw him a sharp glance. "No time fer jokes. The meetin' was serious business. All th' chiefs got together t' figure out some way t' stop all the raidin'. The gangs're cuttin' each other up too much."

"We're doin' okay," somebody said.

"So far," Al answered. "Y'know those Muslims uptown . . . they're all bunched up t'gether now in one big super-gang. Got a leader they call Timmy Jim."

"Them black bastards."

"Yeah," Al agreed. "So far they been pretty quiet. But if they start movin' all together, and us white gangs're all split up, the way things are now—we're dead meat."

Everyone started muttering.

"So we gotta start workin' t'gether," Al said.

Dino shook his head. "How we know we can trust the other gangs?"

"How they know they can trust us?" Al shot back. "I'll tell ya how—we're gonna start out small. We're gonna let Ron start fixin' stuff for some of the other gangs. And th' Chelsea gang agreed t' let us use th' stuff in their warehouses.

Ron can go there an' they'll let him take what he wants. No more raids on 'em. And they won't raid us."

"That don't smell right," someone else said. "Them Chelsea rats always been hittin' us. Ever since I was a kid."

Al said, "Well, we're gonna try and see if we can get along together. It's worth a try."

"It's a trap," Dino said. "You got suckered by some sweet talk."

Al walked straight up to Dino. He was shorter and skinnier than Dino, but it was Dino who backed a step away. "Lissen speedie," Al said, "you wanna fight so bad, go uptown and fight th' Muslims."

Dino's face went red. "Aww . . . don't get hopped up. I was only—"

"You was shootin' off yer mouth," Al said. "As usual. Only time you keep it closed is when it's fulla pills."

Dino said nothing. But his face went dark with hatred.

And that was that. Ron started fixing machinery for other gangs, working longer hours and sleeping even less than he had before. Most times the other gang members would come into Gramercy turf under a white flag of truce, carrying the equipment they wanted fixed. Soon, when they saw how well Ron worked, they began asking him to come to their turfs to fix equipment that was too big for them to carry.

Ron began to move around the area, going into different turfs. Al put only one restriction on him: he was not allowed to fix guns for any other gang. Wherever Ron went, he was always accompanied by at least one other gang member. A warrior. And, usually, by Davey as well. He fixed generators and freezers, heaters and stoves, truck engines and street lamps. Once he even repaired an old movie projector in an empty, crumbling theater for a gang that had films to show.

Each of the gangs was very much like the Gramercy Association. Teen-aged guys and girls, a few smaller kids. Hardly any older people; no one over thirty. The City hadn't been closed, officially, long enough for the gang kids to get that old. Also, gang life wasn't conducive to old age. Everyone was poor, dirty, without education, without decent food, without medicines—it was like living in the Middle Ages. The constant raids had also helped to kill off many of the youngest and strongest warriors. But Al was working desperately to maintain the shaky truce that he had helped establish among the gangs.

One day Ron was walking back from an area called the East Village, after fixing a building's heater. He passed a dozen kids Davey's age playing on the littered, cracked sidewalk. They were running and laughing, making lots of noise, breathless happy grins on their dirty faces.

*How can they be happy?* Ron wondered. *In the middle of all this, how can they laugh?* Then he realized that the children didn't know any other world. *They're like kids everywhere. All they want is a chance to live.*

Then he saw that they were playing a war game, fighting a make-believe battle with sticks or fingers for guns. Feeling sick inside, Ron knew that none of those children would ever see thirty.

There were adults in the city, Ron discovered. Up in the market area, along Broadway above Times Square. You could buy food there, and clothes, and other things. This was the black market, with stalls set up on the sidewalks offering goods smuggled in from outside the Dome.

Walking along Broadway, under the sagging blank theater marquees, Ron passed long wooden counters heaped high with canned foods, clothes new and used, gadgets of all sorts, and even some jewelry. Behind the counters were adults, men mostly. Some of them were really old, Ron saw. As old as his father. He bought tools that he needed from some of these aging men. He saw that they all carried guns and had young assistants at their sides all the time; the assistants were also armed.

You needed money in the market. No bartering, no trading. Just cash. That's why the kids worked so hard for money during the summer. The only way to get food after the city was officially closed for the year was to buy it at the market, or steal it from another gang. No gang had enough money to buy all the food it needed, not when a tiny can of peas cost five dollars. Ron suddenly realized that somebody on the Outside was getting rich off the teen-aged gangs.

*They smuggle food into the City and make a fortune doing it,* Ron told himself. *It's all carefully organized and smoothly operated. Everybody profits . . . except the kids.*

And the kids were almost always hungry. Ron knew that he was losing weight, getting as skinny and mean-looking as Dino or Al or any of the others. Even Sylvia was beginning to look gaunt, and she ate better than most. It wasn't yet winter, either.

Ron had heard stories about gang raids on the market area.

Soldiers had suddenly appeared inside the Dome, killing mercilessly, burning whole sections of the City where the gangs lived. *Even the Army is part of the system.*

Ron saw Sylvia just about every day. She smiled at him, talked with him, let it show very clearly that she liked him. But Ron never touched her, never even let himself get within arm's reach of her. He wanted to hold her and love her again. Instead, he kept his distance.

When they talked, it was mostly about non-dangerous topics. Like Davey.

"He's helping me a lot," Ron would say. "He'll be a good mechanic someday."

And she would reply, "You oughtta see his room. He's got it filled with stuff. Looks like th' junkyards down by th' river."

True to Al's word, the Chelsea gang let Ron roam through their warehouses and take anything he wanted. But when Ron couldn't find things he needed there, he had to go up to the market area and search for them. If he could find what he wanted, he had to pay cash for it.

Dino didn't like that at all. "He's spendin' money we need for food!" he complained.

Al snapped back, "We get th' money back from th' gang Ron buys the stuff for."

Dino shook his head and muttered something.

"We gotta work t'gether with the other gangs, an' stop fightin' among outselves," Al repeated to the gang council. The kids sat on the gravel of the rooftop in the evening darkness. They didn't say much, and it was too dark to see their faces and figure out if they really agreed with Al or not.

Doggedly, Al went on trying to convince them. "Those Muslims uptown are *organized*. We gotta be jes' as strong as they are or they'll come down here and pick us off, one gang at a time."

"Bullshit," somebody said in the darkness. It sounded to Ron like Dino.

"That's the way we're gonna do things," Al said firmly, "as long as I'm runnin' this gang."

The meeting broke up soon after, and the guys started filing down the stairs to their rooms for the night. Ron went up to Al.

"Maybe I shouldn't buy things at the market. Maybe I should just tell the other gangs that if we can't find what we need in the warehouses—"

"No," Al said sharply. "Long as we're not really takin' money we need for food, why should we stop?"

"Well, Dino—"

"Dino can go suck his thumb."

Ron said, "He's going to make trouble for you."

"I know," Al answered quietly. With a shake of his head, he said, "Someday I'll hafta stop him. Before he stops me."

Then he walked past Ron and went to the stairs, leaving Ron standing there alone on the roof, wishing very much that he could be somewhere else, somewhere where he could see the stars and not be so close to death.

Al started letting Ron go to the market area alone, or with no one accompanying him except Davey. Dino protested, of course, and claimed that Ron would run away and hide. But Al overruled him.

Ron liked the market area. It was a connection with the world Outside, the safe, sane world of the Tracts and his parents and friends and the Exams and peace and plenty. *The world that supplies this black market and lets the kids stay in here and die*, he reminded himself.

The market area was busy and noisy, almost like the City during the summer tourist season, except that there were no cars or buses in the streets. And the people roaming the sidewalks were mostly kids, dressed in rags.

The adults who ran the sidewalk stands were dressed much better. Standing behind their makeshift wooden tables, heaped high with goods for sale, the adults looked well fed, even over-weight. They were clean and healthy. Their eyes were clear and alert. They went home to Tracts outside the Dome every night and watched their own children growing fat and clean and healthy.

But there was one hardware merchant who seemed almost as raggedly dressed as the kids themselves. Ron got to know him fairly well, since he had the best collection of tools and machinery parts in the entire market area.

His name was Dewey, and he was an old man with a rough gray beard and a million tiny wrinkled lines around his eyes. His hair was gray too, almost white. But it was still thick and shaggy. His eyes were very light blue, and almost always looked sad. He was big and burly, with a thick heavy body—strong not fat, powerful arms, and hands that were large and tough. Even though he seemed very old, Ron thought he could handle Dino or even Al without much trouble.

Just about every week Ron would go to the market. He'd push and worm his way through the yelling, arguing crowds of kids who clustered around the food counters and walk quickly down the side street where there weren't as many kids and everything was quieter. They sold clothes here, and tools. Finally, Ron would come to Dewey's hardware counter.

The old man was almost always perched on a rickety wooden stool, looking as if he were half-asleep. But when he saw Ron, he'd smile and talk for hours.

"Yep," he said, one afternoon, "I been watchin' you for just about two months now. Not many kids come around this end of the market. Too many of 'em working out how to kill one another, not enough of 'em caring about how to build things up."

Ron felt almost embarrassed, standing there in front of the wooden sidewalk counter. Dewey smiled back at him from the other side, leaning back dangerously on his stool.

"I . . . well, I'm really from Outside," Ron mumbled. "I got stuck here at the end of the summer."

The old man's shaggy eyebrows lifted a bit. "Oh? That so? Huh! You're not the first one to get caught in that net. Dyin' to get out, I suppose?"

Ron nodded. "Guess so."

"Wish I could help you," Dewey said. "I can't get out my—"

The rumble of a truck's engine stopped him in the middle of his words. Ron heard it, too. He turned to look down the street.

"Who's still got gas for trucks?" Ron wondered out loud.

"Muslims," Dewey said. His voice sounded funny. Not scared or even worried. Just grim.

An open-backed pickup truck nosed around the corner and drove slowly down the street toward them. Ron could see two black kids in the cab and another black standing in back with a rifle in his hands. Another truck followed the first one. And then another.

"Get back here," Dewey said.

Without even thinking of arguing, Ron went behind the counter.

"Inside." Dewey jerked a thumb toward the door of the building that his stand was in front of. "Get inside and don't come out 'til I tell you."

Ron glanced at the advancing trucks and then looked at the old man. His face was completely serious. Ron went to the doorway and pushed on the metal and glass door. It swung smoothly and Ron stepped into the shadows inside the building. He found himself in a lobby, almost like the lobby of the hotel he had stayed in so many weeks earlier.

He looked back through the door and saw truck after truck rumbling past. Each was empty in back except for one black youth with a gun of some sort. Ron stopped counting after twenty trucks had gone by, but still more came.

Dewey stood behind his counter and watched them without moving. When the last truck had passed, he turned and pushed through the doorway to where Ron was standing.

"You said you're with the Gramercy gang?" Dewey asked.

"Yes."

"Well, you won't be getting back there today. Better stay with me tonight."

"If there's going to be trouble . . ."

Dewey shrugged. "The Muslims did this last year, just before the summer season opened up. There was a lot of trouble then."

"Did what? What's going on?"

"The Muslims don't come into the market like you kids do. They come in force, like an invading army. They stay for a day or two, load up all their trucks with what they want, then they go back uptown. Last year they took over the whole market for a couple days, and the white gangs went wild. They fought a big battle down on Thirty-eighth Street—"

"But why?"

Dewey made a sour face. "White and black don't mix. Don't ask me why, they just don't. These white kids just go crazy when they see the Muslims—crazy . . . Funny thing is, the Muslims treat us pretty fair here in the market. They pay fair prices for whatever they take. Of course, *they* decide what's fair, and if they think you're tryin' to cheat them . . ." Dewey shook his head.

"Then I'm stuck here for as long as they're around?" Ron asked.

Nodding, Dewey said, "It's best not to get in their way. There's bound to be trouble and you never know where it's going to start. You can stay with me tonight. I live right upstairs here."

**R**on stayed in the cool shadows of the lobby all afternoon, watching the street outside.

The lobby had once been beautiful. But now its marble walls were cracked and stained. Sliding doors that had once opened onto gleaming sleek elevators now hung crookedly, halfway open. The elevator shafts were dark and empty.

Outside on the street things were very quiet. Dewey sat on his stool for a long time, looking up the street, squinting in the slanting afternoon sunlight. Ron couldn't see what he was watching.

Then a patrol of black warriors came past and stopped at Dewey's counter. They were dressed no better than any of the white gang kids, but somehow they looked sharper, more *together*. Like they had an exact job to do, and they knew how to do it well.

Ron had never seen blacks close-up before. Not at home. No

blacks lived in any of the housing Tracts he knew of. The only blacks he had ever seen had been soldiers on TV.

These kids looked serious and alert. But they weren't afraid to laugh. One of them cracked a joke that Ron couldn't hear, and it broke all of them up. Even Dewey was laughing. After watching them for a while, Ron wondered what all the fuss was about. These were ordinary guys, acting pretty much the way anybody would act. Except that each of them carried a rifle slung over his shoulder, and even Dewey seemed to fear something about them.

The long day finally ended. Ron was sitting on the steps at the end of the lobby when Dewey pushed the front door open and came in, wiping sweat from his face with a red and white kerchief.

"You'd best bunk in with me tonight. The Muslims might give you trouble if they found you in the streets."

Standing up, Ron asked, "Can I help you bring your stuff inside?"

Dewey glanced back at the counter outside, with its hardware and machinery parts scattered over it.

"No, we won't have to. Not today. That's one of the good things about the Muslims. Nobody steals when they're in the market. They themselves don't steal, and if they catch anybody else at it, they shoot him, quick and simple."

Ron let his breath out in a low whistle.

"Besides," Dewey said, "if we take the stuff in, they'll think I don't trust them. Might start a fuss." He clapped Ron's shoulder. "Come on, we've got some climbing to do."

"What floor do you live on?"

"Tenth."

Ron thought that they would simply have to climb ten flights of stairs. It wasn't that easy.

They went up the first two flights. The stairway was not lighted and there were no windows, so Ron followed Dewey as the old man trudged slowly up the steps. *He knows his way even in the dark*, Ron thought.

"Hold it now," Dewey said when they reached the foot of the third flight. "Stay close against the wall on your right. Halfway up this flight there's five broken steps. If you're not careful you'll fall through and break your back."

So they slinked against the wall. It felt rough and gritty. On the next flight they had to do the same thing, only this time they kept on the left side.

"Why don't you fix these stairs?" Ron asked. "I can do it for you if—"

Dewey laughed in the darkness. "After I worked so hard to set 'em up this way?"

"What?"

"Think I want visitors bustin' in on me while I'm asleep?" the old man said, still chuckling.

There were traps and barricades on every flight. At the eighth floor, Dewey pulled Ron into one of the rooms. By the last glimmerings of late-afternoon light filtering through a grimy window, Ron saw that there was a rope ladder hanging from a hole in the ceiling.

"It's monkey style from here on," Dewey said, as he grabbed

the rope in one hand. "The stairs are out completely from here up to the tenth floor."

They went up the rope ladder. Dewey climbed heavily, slowly. Ron could hear him grunting and puffing. When they reached the top of the ladder, Dewey hauled it up, hand over hand, and coiled it on the floor.

"Here we are," he said.

The landing looked like a little fortress. There were two machine guns sitting on tripods, cases of ammunition and grenades, and a dozen automatic rifles stacked against the wall.

"Nobody gets up here unless I invite 'em," Dewey said proudly.

"Have you ever . . . had anybody . . ."

"Tried to break in on me? Sure. But not for a long while. The word gets around. All them other merchants, they all slink out of the Dome at night, like rats going back to their nests. But I stay here. I live here. All the time. And if you can't defend yourself, you'd best not try it."

Dewey's apartment was a staggering surprise. It was big, roomy, and beautiful. The lights went on as soon as they stepped into the living room, and Ron could hear the soft whine of a well-maintained generator running somewhere not too far away.

"It's like a palace!"

"Ought to be," Dewey said. "I've got the whole floor to myself. And I've spent twenty years fixing everything up just the way I like it."

There was a carpet on the floor; not as rich or as thick as those Ron had known back home, but it was clean and well kept. The living room was filled with real furniture—sofas and soft chairs. One whole wall was lined with bookshelves, and there wasn't an empty space to be seen.

"No TV," Ron muttered.

"Can't get TV broadcasts here inside the Dome," Dewey said, "except in the summer, when they pipe 'em in from Outside."

Dewey excused himself for a few minutes, leaving Ron alone to wander around the big living room. Looking at the books, the furniture, the big clean windows with real curtains on them, suddenly Ron felt his eyes filling with tears. It was like home! The home he would never see again. He had almost forgotten what it was like to be in a comfortable room with real chairs and a sofa.

Dewey came back into the living room, cleanly washed and wrapped in a gorgeous blue robe. "I have to wear my old clothes down on the street or the kids would start to get ideas about how rich I am," he explained. "But up here I can dress like a gentleman."

Ron just stood there, blinking away tears and feeling stupid.

An uncomfortable look crossed Dewey's face. "Go on in and take a bath while I fix dinner," he said gruffly.

For the first time in months, Ron sank into hot water and scrubbed himself clean. He never realized that ordinary soap could smell so good.

And Dewey's dinner was the best Ron had eaten since coming into the Dome. Even better than the restaurants. The old man drank wine with his dinner and had glass after glass of brandy afterward.

"My one vice," he said to Ron, holding his glass up crookedly over his head for a moment.

They went back into the living room and sat side by side on the big sofa. Dewey brought his glass and brandy bottle with him. He put the bottle on the table beside the sofa, next to him.

It was night outside now, but through the sweeping windows at the far end of the room, Ron could see little pinpoints of light here and there in the otherwise darkened city, like tiny stars in the unending blackness of space.

"See anything?" Dewey asked, squinting at the windows.

"Just a couple of lights," Ron said. "Don't you see them?"

Shaking his head, the old man answered, "No. I can't see very much anymore. I'm going blind."

"Blind?"

"Yup. In another year or so I'll be blind as a mole. I have to make sure I keep everything in here exactly in place, so I don't bump into things."

Ron didn't know what to say.

"The City," Dewey said, leaning back on the sofa. "She used to be ablaze with light! Outshone all the stars in the sky!" He was suddenly shouting. "Lights everywhere. The Great White Way. All gone . . . dead and gone."

There were tears in the old man's eyes.

"How did it happen?" Ron asked. "Were you here when they closed the City?"

"You never saw her the way she was, boy. You're too young. I was here. She was a beautiful city. Beautiful—but sick. Corrupt and dirty."

He took a huge swallow of brandy. "Damn city just got dirtier and sicker and sicker and dirtier. Every day was worse. People died from the poisons in the air. Nobody did their jobs, they just argued and went on strike and fought everybody else. City ran out of money, had to sell its soul to Albany and Washington. They put that stupid Dome up to make things better and it just made everything worse. Everybody was going crazy. You couldn't walk down the street without getting shot at."

He finished his glass and reached for the bottle. "Too many people crowded too close together. People started falling over in the streets, dead from pollution or mugging or just plain brain fever. The Mayor was busy running for President. The City Council was busy stuffing its pockets with money and arguing with the unions. The banks threw up their hands and said the city was a bad investment. Eight million bad investments. Then the Federal Health people came in and said the environment inside the Dome had sunk below the level needed to sustain human life. Inside of a year everybody would be dead."

"Wow!" said Ron.

"You should have seen the rush! It was like a riot and an earthquake and a war, all at once. Went on for months. Families separated. Kids left behind. Banks closing their doors, and mobs breakin' 'em down, only to find their money'd been taken out long ago. People running every which way. When the dust finally cleared, the City was declared officially abandoned—empty, nobody here. So they sealed it off."

"Then how did you get in? And the others?"

Dewey laughed. "We never left! I sat here and watched 'em

boiling out of the City. I figured I had plenty of time. And anyway, the more of 'em left, the better for me. I'd have the whole City to myself. Pick up a few things the others had left behind."

"Is that how—"

But the old man wasn't listening to Ron. "After a couple months, Manhattan got to be right livable, with everybody gone. I knew there was a few others like me; a couple thousand of us, at least. We never got out of the City, and as far as the Government was concerned, they wasn't going to come in looking for us. They had enough to do, handling the eight million or so who had come screaming out. So the Government wrote us off their records. Officially, I'm dead. You're talking to a dead man!"

"Not really," Ron said.

Dewey shrugged. "Somewhere Outside there's a Government computer with my death certificate coded into its memory banks, signed and official and everything. Just like all the kids that got stuck inside here. Officially, none of us exist. No social security, no IRS identification number, nothing. We don't exist. None of us."

*But I've got an ID record,* Ron insisted to himself. *They know I exist!*

"That was twenty years ago," Dewey said, his voice sinking to a dark muttering. "Had a woman with me then. She was awful pretty. She died the first winter . . . got sick . . . couldn't find a doctor, no medicine . . ."

The old man slumped against the back of the sofa, eyes closed, head down against his chest, empty glass slipping from his thick fingers. Ron took the glass and placed it quietly on the table next to the nearly empty bottle.

"I'll help you to your bed," Ron said softly. He couldn't tell if Dewey was already asleep or not.

"Thanks, but I can make it by myself," the old man replied, without opening his eyes. "Been getting myself to bed without help for twenty years now. Won't be able to do it much longer, though." Dewey's eyes snapped open and he stared at Ron fiercely. "Tell you what. How'd you like to be my partner? I'm getting too old to keep alive all by myself. The eyes are getting real bad. You could live right here. We could fix a place upstairs for you, deck it out with furniture . . ."

Without even thinking about it, Ron said, "But I've got to get back to my home. As soon as they open the gates next summer—"

Dewey put a hand on Ron's shoulder. "Son, they're never going to let you out. You're not the first kid to get stuck in here. If you show up at a gate without your ID, you'll go straight to the Tombs. If you're lucky, you'll end up in the Army. If you're lucky."

Ron shook his head stubbornly at the old man, but his mind whispered to him, *Forever. You're going to be stuck in here forever.* He turned and stared out the broad windows at the darkened City, where only a pitiful few glimmers of light broke the darkness. *Forever.*

Dewey showed Ron to a bedroom. The old man walked very straight and sure-footed, in spite of all he had drunk. Ron felt as if he were the one who was staggering.

"Good night, son," Dewey said, leaving Ron at the doorway to a small, clean, and well-lit bedroom.

Ron said, "If . . . if I come here to work with you—live with you—could I bring a girl with me?"

Dewey seemed to hold his breath for a moment or two. Then he let it out with a long sigh. "Some kinds of girls are nothing but trouble, you know."

"She's not like that."

"You sure?"

Nodding, Rod added, "She's got a brother, too. Six or seven years old. He's a good kid. Interested in machinery."

Dewey ran a hand through his shaggy white hair. "I ask for a partner and I get a family. Okay . . . I'm probably crazy, but— bring 'em along. We'll see how it works out."

"Thanks! Thanks an awful lot!"

"Good night. Get some sleep," Dewey said. He started to turn away, then he looked back at Ron. "You're really sure now?"

"About Sylvia?"

"About our partnership. You'll come back? You won't disappoint an old man?"

"I'll come back," Ron said firmly. "Don't worry."

**R**on stayed with Dewey all the next day. Toward evening, the Muslims' trucks started to pull out of the market area. They were loaded with food and supplies. A smudge of smoke rose toward the south, somewhere downtown of the market area, in the direction of the Gramercy turf.

"Trouble," said Dewey. "One of the white gangs must have had a run-in with the Muslims."

The trouble never reached the market area, and the day ended quietly. Dewey insisted that Ron stay with him another night. Ron easily agreed. The old man's food was too good to miss. And sleeping on a real bed again was like being in heaven.

The following morning Ron started for the Gramercy turf. He passed the burned-out section. Buildings were black with smoke. Windows, doors, roofs all gone so that the daylight sifted through the still-smoldering insides of the buildings.

White warriors were patrolling the streets here and there. Either they knew Ron from his earlier trips to the market through their turf, or they didn't care who he was as long as his skin was white.

Turning a corner, Ron saw a handful of kids sitting quietly on the front steps of an old brown stone house. One of them had the stump of a broken knife tucked in his belt. He couldn't have been older than Davey. The children were watching the unmoving body of a boy, about twelve years old, that lay under a swarm of flies in the gutter. The corpse lay face up, chest crumpled and brown with dried blood. His eyes were open and his mouth was twisted as if he had been screaming when he died.

Ron felt his teeth clench. *The local gang ought to clean up after themselves better than that*, he grumbled silently. *Those kids are scared half to death*. Then he thought of his own retching reaction to the first corpse he had seen, back in the truck on that first raid into Chelsea turf. It seemed like a thousand years ago. Ron realized he had changed, hardened. He wasn't certain he liked it.

The Gramercy area looked deserted when Ron got there. There was no damage, no sign that fighting had come this far downtown. But there was no one on the streets, either. Everything looked dead and emptier than usual. As he climbed the steps inside their home building, Ron wondered where everyone had gone. There was no one in the halls. No kids playing. Nobody around anywhere.

He took the stairs three at a time and didn't stop until he was pounding on Sylvia's door. She opened it and went wide-eyed when she recognized him.

"Oh, Ron!" She threw her arms around his neck. "We thought they killed you!"

He kissed her, long and warm and hard, forgetting about Al and Dewey and everything else except her.

Finally she pulled away from him. "Al's called a war meetin'," Sylvia said. "All th' gangs're doin' it. Th' Muslims made a lotta trouble yesterday an' all th' gangs're tryin' to figger out what t' do."

"The hell with them," Ron said. "We're getting out of here."

"Whatcha mean?"

"You and me and Davey. We're getting out. Right now, while they're all busy making war talk. We're going to live in the market, live like real human beings. Get Davey and let's go."

"You're crazy," Sylvia said, backing away from him. "You can't just quit th' gang."

"Yes we can. And we're going to do it right now. Where's Davey?"

But Sylvia was shaking her head. "No, Ron, it won't work. You can't quit a gang. They'll come after you and kill you. They'll find you, wherever you go. Nobody's allowed t' quit."

Ron stood in the doorway, feeling his face twisting into a frown. "Listen. Nobody owns me. Or you."

"Al went to bat for you," Sylvia said, talking more slowly now, trying to explain. "He letcha into th' gang when he coulda left you out on the street t' die. Right? He hadda go against Dino t' bring you into th' gang. If you buzz off on him now, it'll make things rough for Al. Catch?"

Ron muttered, "I don't owe him—"

"He saved your *life*, Ron!"

Ron slapped a hand against his leg. "Does that mean that he owns me? And you?"

She shrugged. "It means you can't quit th' gang. Unless he says it's okay."

"And you? If he lets me go, will you come with me?"

"Al won't lemme go." She looked away from Ron.

He reached out and touched Sylvia's shoulder. "But if he was willing to let you go, would you come with me?"

She wouldn't look at him. She stared down at the floor.

Ron lifted her chin with his outstretched hand until she was gazing right at him. "Would you?" he asked.

In a voice so low that he could barely hear it, Sylvia said, "Yes."

Ron smiled at her. "Okay. I guess I'd better get to that war meeting, then."

"Don't do anything that'll hurt Al in front of Dino," Sylvia called to him as he started for the steps.

The roof was packed with guys, warriors and others that Ron had never seen before. As Ron edged through the door to join the crowd, he could hear Dino shouting: "Them Muslims been gettin' too smart for their own damned good! It's time we taught 'em a lesson!"

"Yeah!"

"Right on!"

"Hell yeah!"

Then one of the guys standing next to Ron suddenly called out, "Hey look who' here! The fix-it dude!"

Everyone turned toward Ron. Through the sea of faces Ron could see Al up at the head of the crowd. He was almost smiling, as if he was really glad to see Ron.

"Hey, Ron, we thought you was killed."

Ron wormed his way up to the front of the crowd. "No, I'm all right. I stayed . . ." *Don't tell them who you stayed with!* Ron warned himself. "Uh . . . I stayed in the market area, hid out until the Muslims left. I hear there was trouble."

"I hear there was trouble," Dino sing-songed, trying to make Ron's words sound funny. "Humpin' *right* there was trouble. And there's gonna be more. Right?"

"Right!" answered half a dozen guys.

"Cool it," Al snapped. "Ron, we thought the Muslims killed you. But since they didn't maybe we don't have any real reason for fightin' against 'em."

"No reason!" Dino shouted. "Them black bastards gonna take over th' whole humpin' city if we don't stop 'em!"

Al made a sour face. "We ain't gonna stop 'em by runnin' crazy. Dontcha think they're ready for us right now? Waitin' for us?"

"Half th' gangs between here and th' market are ready t' fight," Dino argued. "We gonna jus' sit here?"

"Be smarter if we wait 'til *all* th' gangs between here and th' market are ready to march t'gether," Al said. "An' all th' midtown gangs, too."

"No!" Dino yelled. "I say we fight 'em now. An' if yer too chicken t' fight, then I'll take th' gang with me!"

Al stayed unruffled. But his eyes blazed. "Dino, you got such hot rocks t' fight th' Muslims, go fight 'em. But the Gramercy gang don't declare war on nobody without a vote."

Dino stood there looking like a volcano about to blow its top. His face was getting redder and redder.

Al said, "You wanna take a vote?"

"No!" Dino snarled. "I don't need no vote. I'm goin' with whoever starts after the Muslims. An' there's plenny guys here who'll go with me. Right?"

This time only a few voices answered, "Right."

"Go on then," Al said calmly. "Anytime you wanna. An' you can come back anytime, too. But th' Gramercy gang ain't declarin' war on nobody. Not today."

Dino stamped off, pushing through the crowd. He kicked the door open and disappeared down the stairs. The meeting started to break up. Guys began drifting toward the door in groups of two or three, talking among themselves.

Ron waited until everybody else had left the roof, and he was alone with Al.

Al's tired face almost smiled at him. "I'm glad yer okay. We got plenty worried when you didn't show up an' we heard th' Muslims had taken over th' market. You see Sylvia? She was pretty shook up about you."

Nodding, Ron said, "I saw her."

"Okay."

For a moment, Ron didn't know what to say or do. There was something in Al's eyes, those old-man's eyes set into his young face, something that Ron couldn't fathom.

Finally he blurted, "Al, I want to leave the gang."

"Leave? Whaddaya mean?"

Ron told him about Dewey. "I'd still work for you, for the gang. I'd fix anything you want, anytime you want. For free."

But Al was frowning. "Can't letcha go. Too much stirrin' right now. Gangs ain't supposed t' let guys quit. It's a bad thing. 'Specially right now, with this Dino crap an' th' Muslims an' all." He shook his head. "The answer's gotta be no."

Ron asked, "Suppose I stay a member of the gang, but just live in the market area, with this old guy. How would that be?"

"I dunno," Al said slowly. "I gotta think about it . . . later, after all this trouble settles down."

With a shrug, Ron said, "Okay. Later." *Don't even mention Sylvia to him. Don't even think about it!*

Ron started for the door that led downstairs. Al called to him, "Hey, don't take off on yer own, now, unnerstand? I'd just hafta send a coupla guys t' drag ya back. Don't make me do that."

Ron nodded. "I won't."

Al studied him for a long, silent moment. "I'm sorry it's gotta be this way."

"So am I," Ron said.

That night Ron's sleep was filled with dreams. He dreamed of Dewey, of Al, of the dark somber Muslims walking through the streets of the market area with their rifles slung over their shoulders. He dreamed of Sylvia. Mostly of her.

He dreamed that she was crying. Then Davey started screaming.

Ron's eyes snapped open. It wasn't a dream. Davey *was* screaming!

It was still dark. Davey screamed again, a high, thin screech of pain and terror.

Ron leaped from his mattress, pulled on his pants as he ran, and raced downstairs to Sylvia's room. The door was open, the lights were on.

Sylvia was kneeling beside her mattress with a torn sheet wrapped around her. She was crying and holding Davey in her arms. The boy had stopped screaming, but he was crying now too, with quick panic-filled gulping sobs. Sylvia rocked back and forth with Davey's curly black hair nestled against her breast.

Ron knelt beside her. Her lip was split and bleeding. There was an ugly bruise on her throat.

Then he saw Davey. The boy's face had four straight red welts across one check—finger marks. One eye was swollen. He was trembling, shaking with terror, whimpering.

"Dino," said Sylvia. Her voice was strained, slurred. "He wanted me t' go with him. He's quittin' th' gang. Started slappin' me around when I wouldn't go with him . . . Davey tried t' protect me an' he beat up on Davey. Kicked him . . ."

Ron found that he was shaking now. He turned and found Al coming in. There were more people out in the hallway.

Barely able to control himself, Ron got to his feet and went to the door. He pushed through the growing crowd in the hallway and raced upstairs. On his worktable was an automatic pistol. In fifteen seconds he had clicked all its parts together, worked the action twice to make sure it was ready to fire, and then started back downstairs.

Ammunition was in a storeroom on the second floor. His hands steady now, his insides white-hot, Ron turned on the store-room light and found a box of cartridges for the pistol. When he finished loading the automatic, he jammed the rest of the ammo into his pants pockets. Then he turned toward the door.

Al was standing there watching him.

"Where you goin'?" Al asked.

"Where do you think?" Ron snapped. He was surprised at how calm his voice sounded. Flat. Deadly.

Al shook his head. "No, you ain't. Sylvia an' th' kid ain't dead. They'll be okay."

"I'm going to kill that sonofa—"

"Dino'll kill you before you even know where he is," Al said. "Dontcha think he's waitin' for ya right now? He knows you'll be out after him, an' he's waitin'. With a big grin on his stupid face."

Ron stood there, smoldering like a hot ember.

"Put the ammo back," Al said, "an' put th' gun away. Dino's left an' he won't be back. That's the end of it."

"But my ID card . . ."

"That's the end of it," Al repeated, his voice stronger.

*Not for me*, Ron told himself. *It's not the end of it for me*. But he turned back and did what Al commanded.

I t was more than a week before Al let Ron go to the market again. And when he did, he ordered two warriors to go with Ron.

"Jes' in case you meet up with Dino," Al said, "or there's more trouble with th' Muslims."

*Or I try to run away*, Ron added silently.

At the market, Ron told Dewey what had happened. All of it. The old man listened patiently as he sat on his stool behind the counter full of hardware. Once in a while he nodded or scratched his beard.

"So maybe I can get away later on," Ron said at last, "but not now."

Dewey's eyes looked sadder than usual. "I should've figured that the gang wouldn't let you go. Especially with all this trouble with the Muslims."

"More trouble?"

Nodding, Dewey answered, "Some of the mid-town gangs tried a few raids on Muslim turf. Wouldn't be surprised if this Dino fella wasn't in on it."

"What happened?"

"Don't know, exactly. Except that a lot of kids came through here yesterday. Most of 'em were hurt pretty bad. Looked like the Muslims chewed 'em up fierce."

Ron shook his head. "I'll get free of the gang," he said, his voice low. "I promise."

"Don't take any chances you don't have to take," Dewey said. "I can wait. I waited a long time to find a boy like you, son. I can wait a few months longer."

Feeling sad and embarrassed, Ron covered up his emotions with, "Well . . . don't worry. I can take care of myself."

"Sure," said Dewey. "I know."

"I'll see you."

"So long, son. Good luck."

Life settled into a tense routine. It was getting to be winter now, and even though the Dome protected the city from the fiercest winds and bitterest cold, it got too chilly to walk the streets without a coat. The buildings that the kids lived in were heated only when they had enough fuel oil to run the furnaces. Otherwise they made wood fires at night out of furniture, doors, anything they could find that would burn. The smoke hung in the air inside the Dome, making Ron's eyes sting and his lungs burn from coughing.

Slowly, the other gangs stopped asking for Ron to repair

things for them. They even stopped bringing in small repair jobs for him.

"They're runnin' low on food an' money," Al said. "Got nothin' left t' trade with."

Ron saw all the work he had done for the Gramercy kids become meaningless. The lights, the stoves, the electrical machinery he had fixed—all were useless now. Even the generator down in the basement, which warriors had died for, was now cold and silent, without fuel. It couldn't snow inside the Dome, of course, but the winter cold seeped in, bringing at first discomfort, then pain, and finally sickness.

The bruises that Dino had put on Sylvia and Davey slowly faded away. But Davey stopped going out on the streets to play with the other boys his own age. He developed a hoarse, dry cough that got deeper and more racking every day. The child stayed close to Ron almost all the time, and even slept with him many nights, under as big a pile of blankets as they could find. Still, Davey coughed and Ron always awoke shivering.

There was no news about Dino. At the market area, there were plenty of stories about raids around the border of the Muslim turf. Sometimes it was white gangs hitting the Muslims, sometimes the Muslims raiding the whites. The fighting was bitter. Many were killed and wounded.

The shaky truce that Al had engineered among the white gangs was beginning to crumble. Kids who were cold and hungry were no longer willing to live in peace if they thought they could get the food or fuel they needed by force. There was no fighting in the Gramercy area though. Ron concluded that the other gangs respected Al too much for them to attack his gang.

Then the night exploded.

Ron was asleep when the first blast lifted him off his mattress. He bounced on the floor, completely awake and totally scared. More blasts! People shouting, cursing, screaming.

Ron's mind began to work. *It's a raid!*

Scrambling to his feet, he dashed out of the room and downstairs. A thin, oily-smelling smoke drifted up the stairwell. Guys were dashing all around down on the first floor. Ron stopped at the second floor landing. More warriors were bunched up in the doorway to the ammo room. Al was in there, shouting orders.

Ron heard glass break downstairs and then a sheet of flame *whooshed* up from the first floor. Screams of agony came up the stairs with the blistering heat and glaring white flames.

"Up on th' roof!" Al shouted. "Quick!"

They all boiled upstairs, heading for the roof. Ron still heard shouts down below as warriors pounded past him on the stairs. There was shouting out on the street. Flames were licking up the stairs now, as Ron stood frozen watching them. He heard the shouts of excited, victory-crazed guys mixed with the shrieks of those who were burning to death.

Ron could feel the heat singeing his face, curling the hair on his hands and arms. All at once he turned and ran upstairs. Not for the roof. For Sylvia's room. He pushed her door open. The rest of the guys kept on swarming toward the roof.

By the flickering light of the flames he could see her sitting huddled in the farthest corner of the room, covering Davey with her arms.

"Shh . . . shhh . . . don't cry. Davey, please don't cry."

The boy was rigid with fright. His eyes were squeezed shut and he clung to Sylvia so hard that Ron knew he must be hurting her.

"Sylvia!" he called.

She looked up. "Oh, Ron, what're we gonna do?"

"Come on. They're all going up to the roof."

He helped Sylvia to her feet. "Give Davey to me," he said.

She shook her head. "Naw, I'll hold him."

Ron stroked Davey's hair as they headed for the doorway. "It's okay, Davey. It's me, Ron. We'll be okay. Don't be scared."

The fire was roaring two flights below them and licking up the stairwell. Ron could feel its searing heat on his back as they started up the steps. They passed his own floor and were heading up the last flight of stairs that led to the roof when the shooting started again.

This time the shots came from the roof. The screaming and swearing was almost as loud as the gunfire. Ron heard heavy machine guns blasting the night air. *They were waiting up on the roof for us! It's a trap!*

The door burst open and two warriors staggered down the steps, bleeding, limping, hands empty and eyes glazed with pain and shock. Then a girl stumbled through the doorway, covered with blood. She collapsed and tumbled halfway down the stairs. Sylvia buried her face in Davey's dark hair. Two warriors pushed past Ron and headed down the steps in panic.

"My room, quick!" Ron whispered to Sylvia. Numbly, she followed him. The fire was only one floor below them now. The stairway and landing were lit by its hungry red glow. More shots rang out from the roof.

The only window in Ron's room opened onto an air shaft. There was a chance that they could get down to the bottom of it and sneak into the next building, then hide there until the battle was over.

In the flickering shadows, Ron slashed blankets and mattress coverings and knotted them together with shaking fingers into one long rope. Looping one end around Sylvia's shoulders, he lowered her and Davey out the window and to the bottom of the air shaft.

The fire was licking at his doorway, evil and hungry. The smoke was making him cough, blurring his vision. Ron tied his end of the makeshift rope to an ancient steam radiator that hadn't worked for twenty years. He hoped it wouldn't fall apart under his weight. Then, coughing and teary-eyed, he crawled out the window and edged down the side of the building.

He almost made it all the way before the rope broke. He landed hard, but on his feet, then sank to all fours. Looking up, he saw flames spurt from his own window.

He turned and saw Sylvia kneeling a few feet away from him, still clutching Davey close to her. Without a word he grabbed her and led them across the grimy, garbage-slick shaftway to the next building. Ron kicked in a window and stepped through into a pitch-dark room. He helped Sylvia and Davey through.

They groped in the flame-lit dimness away from the fire. For the first time, Ron realized that the monstrous blaze was roaring; the sound had just not penetrated his consciousness until that moment. Over its hideous roar, he could hear more shots and screams.

They made their way down to the basement and hid behind an old, broken-down furnace. Things scuttled across the floor in the darkness. Ron wasn't worried about roaches or mice, particularly. He saw the red glowing eyes of big rats, though, and knew that he wouldn't be able to sleep.

Not that he could have, anyway. From outside he could hear more shots, then nothing for a long time except the gradually diminishing roar of the fire. Then came a huge crashing groan that Ron guessed was their building caving in from the gutting flames. He heard shouting and laughing.

In the darkness, Ron couldn't see Sylvia's face or Davey's. But he heard the boy whimpering, a high-pitched thin crying sound of pure terror. Sylvia kept whispering, "Shhh . . . shhh" and tried to hold Davey close to her, so that his voice would be muffled. But Ron could still hear it.

As morning came, Ron saw that there were windows in the basement, set high up in the walls. He went to one of them and carefully peeked outside, standing on tiptoe.

The street outside was covered with bodies. Warriors mostly, but there were several girls among them. Some of them were blackened with burns. Others were torn by bullets. All of them were dead.

A group of warriors was slowly coming down the street, rifles in their hands. Ron recognized one of them as a member of the Chelsea gang, a kid who had stayed with him whenever he went through the Chelsea warehouses. Striding down the street beside him, grinning happily, was Dino.

Ron's insides suddenly felt as if someone had lit a fire in him. He gripped the edge of the basement window ledge so hard that his fingernails bit into the dust-caked cement.

*If only I had a gun . . .* Then Ron thought of Sylvia and Davey, still huddled behind the furnace. There was nothing he could do. Nothing but watch.

The Chelsea warriors stopped at one of the bodies. It was lying face-down on the sidewalk. Dino nudged the body with the toe of his boot. *My boot!* Ron thought furiously.

Dino pushed the body over onto its back. It was Al. Ron sagged against the gritty basement wall.

"That's him," he heard Dino say. "Good."

Sick with anger and sadness, Ron made his way back to the furnace. Sylvia was sitting against its sooty black metal side, half-asleep. Davey was still in her arms, his eyes still squeezed shut, still whimpering.

Sylvia opened her eyes as Ron sat on the floor beside her. She looked completely exhausted.

"It was the Chelsea gang," Ron said quietly. "Dino's with them."

She didn't move, didn't say anything.

"They got Al. He's dead."

Sylvia looked at him. "Yer sure?"

"I saw his body."

She nodded. Nothing else. No tears, no words. Only a nod.

They sat there for a long, long time. Ron didn't know what

to do. The only sound was Davey's muffled crying.

Slowly Ron realized that the boy was saying a word, one single word over and over again:

"Mommy . . . Mommy . . . Mommy."

Ron stared at the boy, then at Sylvia. She was rocking Davey now, bending her head low over his and whispering into his ear: "It's all right, Davey . . . it's all right . . . I'm here, honey . . . Mommy's here . . ."

"You're . . . you're his mother?" Ron's voice went high with shock.

She looked up at him. "Didn't you know? Al was his father." And now there were tears in her eyes.

**T**he day was cold. Hiding down in the unheated basement, huddling in the dust and dirt, Ron could feel the cold seeping into his bones. Sylvia was dozing. Davey was asleep at last, still in her lap, clinging to her.

Ron went to the window a dozen times an hour. The bodies were still there. The day looked gray and felt damp, as if snow were coming. Of course, inside the Dome no snow ever fell. But it *felt* like a snowy winter day.

Davey woke up late in the afternoon.

"I'm hungry," he whined.

"Shh," Sylvia said. "We gotta wait a while before we can eat."

Ron said to her, "I'll take a look around outside. Maybe I can find something."

"No!" She looked alarmed. "They'll be prowlin' around out there. Wait 'til dark."

Ron waited. It got colder and darker. Sitting there on the cement basement floor, Ron found himself shaking from the cold. They didn't even have coats. Davey had started coughing again. Ron got up and paced around the cluttered basement floor.

"It's dark enough," he whispered to Sylvia at last. "I'm going out."

He might as well have saved his energy.

The gang's main building was completely gutted by the fire. The food supplies, guns, ammo, clothing—all gone. What hadn't burned had been carried away by the victorious Chelsea warriors. Even the dead bodies had been stripped of anything useful or valuable.

There were no people around. None living, that is. The dead bodies littered the streets. And there were the rats. Ron nearly stepped on one before he realized what it was. In the dark, he heard a chittering sound, the *skritch-skritch* of clawed feet scurrying across cement pavement. And he saw the tiny, gleaming, wicked eyes.

A chill raced through him. All thought of food vanished. The previous night, the fire had kept both humans and rats terrified and cowering. Now the rats were out to claim their usual, ultimate victory over the humans. Ron raced back to the basement where he had left Sylvia and Davey. In the darkness, he tripped over a body and sprawled face down on the sidewalk. Something furry brushed against his hand.

Ron nearly screamed. He *did* scream, in his mind. But he managed to keep it silent.

He got to the basement and found them both asleep, untouched.

"Come on, we're going upstairs," Ron said as he shook Sylvia awake.

"Wh . . . whassa matter?"

"Rats."

He could feel the shudder go through her. Silently, they climbed to the top floor of the building and slept on the floor of a bare little room.

But Ron slept very little, only in snatches of a few minutes each. By the time morning started lighting the streets outside, he was wide awake and aching with cold. And he was *hungry*.

Davey was coughing again. And crying.

"Ron, he feels hot. Like he's burnin' up!" Sylvia said.

The child's face was red. Fever.

"He needs food," Sylvia said, her voice close to cracking.

"And medicine," Ron added.

Davey's eyes were still closed, but he was moaning softly, "It hurts . . . hurts . . ."

*Dewey! Dewey will know what to do. He'll have food. And medicine, too, maybe.*

"I've got to get to the market," Ron told her. "I can get food there, and whatever else we need."

"Th' market? You'll never make it that far."

"Yes I will. I've got to."

She reached for his arm. "Ron, don't! You'll get caught. If th' Chelsea gang don't getcha some other gang will. They all know Al's dead by now. They won't give a damn what they do to you!"

He pulled free of her. "I can't sit here and let us starve. Davey needs food and medicine. No way to get them except at the market."

"Ron, wait—"

"I'll be back," he said. "Don't worry about me."

He was out the door before she could say anything else.

It took three days. Ron had to travel slowly, avoiding everybody and anybody on the streets. Most of the day he inched along, a block at a time, sometimes just a building at a time. Ducking into a doorway, he'd look carefully out onto the street and wait until no one was in sight. Then he'd sprint as far as he dared and duck into another doorway, praying that nobody saw him.

Twice he was spotted. Once he simply outran a pack of little kids. He ran until his lungs were aflame and his vision blurred. He raced down one block, cut around a corner, through an alleyway, up a fire-escape ladder, and down the other side of the building. When he collapsed, chest heaving painfully, the kids were nowhere in sight.

Just as night was falling he was surprised by three warriors from a gang he didn't know. Ron stepped into a shadowy doorway and the three of them were already in there. They were just as surprised as he was.

They were smoking something and didn't expect to be disturbed. For a flash of a second the three of them froze, wideeyed, scared. Before they could recover, Ron took off, running wildly again. After a few minutes he looked back over his shoulder. No one was following.

He got to Dewey's place late that night. He nearly forgot about the traps that the old man had set up along the stairs. But he remembered them just in time.

Finally he stood under the hole in the ceiling where the rope ladder had been and yelled out? "Dewey, it's me, Ron. It's Ron! Wake up. Hurry. Please hurry!"

A powerful light suddenly blinded him. He put his hands up over his head to shield himself. The light was blazing bright; Ron could feel its heat.

"You alone?" he heard Dewey's voice ask.

"Yes."

The rope ladder tumbled down and dangled in front of Ron. In a few minutes he was standing in Dewey's living room, trying to tell the old man everything at once.

"Slow down, slow down," Dewey said. "I can't hardly understand you."

Ron took a deep breath and tried to speak more slowly. He told Dewey about Dino, about the raid, the killings, Sylvia and Davey, their need for food and medicine.

Dewey nodded grimly. "Okay. I get the picture."

Then the old man quickly moved through the apartment, pulling a worn old hiking pack from a closet, stuffing it with cans and plastic packages of food, a canteen of water, and cartons of powdered milk. From another closet he took a small metal box marked with a red cross.

"There's penicillin and bug-killers in this kit," he told Ron. "Hope they can do the job, 'cause there's nothing else we can do for him here inside the Dome."

Ron nodded gratefully.

As Ron started to slide his arms through the pack's shoulder harness, Dewey said, "You know you ought to eat something, and get some sleep. You're not goin' to get back for another day anyway, and you look mighty worn out."

Shaking his head, Ron answered, "I can't. That kid might be dying."

Dewey nodded. "I know . . . well, good luck, son."

The old man stuffed handfuls of dried food into Ron's ragged pockets and helped him down to the street. Ron waved to him from the corner, turned, and headed back downtown. He munched on dried piece of fruit as he started out.

It took the rest of that night and all the following day for Ron to get just halfway back to the Gramercy area. He had to be especially careful now because the pack he carried contained valuable property. If anyone saw him, they would kill him just for the chance to look inside the pack. And with the pack weighing him down, Ron couldn't run or fight as well as before.

So he had to go slowly, very slowly, through the dirty, nearly empty streets. Whenever he saw someone or heard anything at all, he hid in an alley or doorway or basement. Most of the day he had to stay hidden. Twice he dozed off while he crouched in basements. Each time he snapped awake, feeling angry at himself and ashamed for being so weak.

He made better time after dark. Still, it was nearly dawn on the third day when he got back to the building where he'd left Sylvia and Davey.

But they weren't in the upstairs room where he had left them. Ron put his pack down on the floor. His shoulders and arms creaked in relief as he got rid of the weight. The room was empty. In the gray light of early morning, Ron searched the whole floor for them. They weren't in any of the rooms.

*She must have gone to look for food*, Ron told himself. *Maybe Davey's feeling better and they both went to look for food.*

But he didn't really believe that.

Ron searched every floor of the building, starting at the top and working down, floor by floor, until he reached the basement. Nothing.

He climbed wearily back up the stairs to the main hallway on the street level.

"Hello dude."

Dino and four Chelsea warriors were standing in the hallway waiting for him. Somehow, Ron wasn't surprised. He almost expected it.

"Lookin' for somebody?" Dino was smiling. A nasty, yellow-toothed smile.

"Where are they?" Ron asked flatly.

Dino laughed. "Where d'ya think? Sylvia came lookin' fer me yesterday. Th' kid was sick an' they both was starvin'. So now she's my girl."

"I'll bet she's thrilled by that."

"You betcha."

Ron jerked a thumb toward the staircase. "I've got medicine for Davey. He—"

"He won't need it. He's dead."

"What?" Ron felt the breath catch in his throat.

With a sour face, Dino said, "Damn' little brat coughed his

guts out all night. Died jes' about an hour ago. One less mouth t' feed."

Without even thinking about what he was doing, Ron growled like an animal and leaped at Dino. He got a glimpse of Dino's face, suddenly scared-looking, and felt the solid shock of their bodies smashing together and hitting the floor. They rolled and thrashed around, and then Ron was on top of Dino, pounding him with both fists.

"Murderer! Butcher!" Ron screamed. Dino's mouth and nose were filled with blood. "Killer! Filthy goddamned killer!"

The other guys pulled Ron off Dino. He fought back, hitting, kicking, screaming at all of them like a cornered wild beast until they clubbed him to his knees and kicked him unconscious.

**R**on came to slowly.

His head throbbed painfully. His body ached and felt stiff. He found that he was lying on the cold floor of a completely dark room. He couldn't see anything at all. No window, no light. Only darkness.

He sat up, taking it easy, trying to see if anything was broken. *Not so bad*, he said to himself. It hurt, but not as much as the first time Dino and his pals had worked him over.

He thought about that time for a moment. It was almost as though the past few months hadn't really happened. Here he was again, stiff and sore from a beating by the same guys. Everything that had happened was like a dream. A bad dream. Al and Davey were dead. As if they had never lived. Nothing but memories now.

Sylvia. Ron frowned, then winced as a cut on his cheek pulled open. *Sylvia. She never gave a damn about me at all*. He almost laughed, but it hurt too much. *Did she really love Al? Or did she do everything just to make sure Davey would get fed and protected? Maybe she went to Dino just to get help for Davey. Sure, that's why she did it. I was gone for three days. She must have thought I wouldn't come back. Maybe she thought I was dead. Dino would be the only one who could help her—and Davey.*

But Ron heard his own voice whisper to him, "Then why is she staying with Dino now? Davey's dead. She doesn't need Dino's help."

He sat there, seeing her face in the darkness, hearing her voice, feeling her touch. He tried to hate her. "You never cared for me at all," he said to her.

Then he thought of Dino, and he *did* hate. Dino had led the raid by the Chelsea gang. He knew all the strong points of the Gramercy headquarters. He knew Al's defenses. Dino had planned the raid. He had triggered the trap. He had killed Al. And Davey too.

Dino was going to kill Ron now. Ron knew it. But he knew one thing more. He knew that he would kill Dino first. He didn't know how he'd do it; he only knew he was going to kill Dino. He snarled like an animal, sitting there in his blackened cage. A few months in the City and Ron had turned into a hating, bloodthirsty animal, eager to kill.

Footsteps outside.

Ron scrambled to his feet, ignoring the pain and stiffness in his body. He had to feel along the walls to find the door, it was that dark in his cell.

From outside he heard a muffled, "Hey, what—" And then scuffling sounds. A thud. A moan. Finally, the rattling of a key in the door's lock.

Ron flattened himself against the wall, next to the door. *When they come in here, I'll jump them.*

But they didn't come in. The door opened outward and somebody flashed a light into the cell. Ron was blinded.

"Hey you! C'mon out, quick! B'fore somebody sees us." It was an urgent whisper.

Ron staggered out of the cell, rubbing his eyes. Squinting in the light from a bare bulb in the ceiling, he found that he was in a hallway. Two guys were standing next to him: strangers. A third guy, one of Dino's pals, was lying face-down on the floor, out cold.

"C'mon, dummy. Move! We're tryin' t' getcha outta here," one of the strangers whispered harshly.

Puzzled, Ron went with them. They led him down the hallway, into a tiny bathroom. They crawled through a window into an alley. Then they sprinted, all three together—Ron and the two strangers—down street after street, staying in the deepest shadows.

After a few blocks, Ron saw a car parked at a corner. The driver must have spotted them at the same moment, because the engine coughed to life.

"Okay, here it is," one of the guys said, panting for breath, as they came up to the car. The rear door swung open and the two guys more-or-less pushed Ron inside.

"Okay," said the driver in a deep, rumbling voice. He handed something to the two guys, who were still standing on the sidewalk beside the car. It looked like a plastic package of white powder.

"This better be the good stuff," one of the guys muttered.

The driver laughed. "It's real, baby. We don't cheat."

He put the car in gear and turned on the headlights. They slid slowly away from the curb and headed up the street, making as little noise as possible. In the faint glow reflected by the dashboard lights, Ron saw that the driver was black.

"What's going on?" Ron asked. "Where are you taking me?"

The driver didn't answer.

They drove in silence for nearly a half-hour, slowly, like a one-car parade. *Or funeral*, Ron thought grimly. They passed the market area heading north. Ron thought he spied the pinpoint of light that was Dewey's home, high up in one of the buildings. As they went through Central Park, Ron saw packs of dogs racing beside the car, barking furiously. He had heard stories about the dogs in the Park. When the City had been officially closed down, many people had turned their pets loose. Thousands of dogs made it to Central Park where they quickly went feral. Now the Park was their own private jungle, and people who wandered in there never came out.

As they left the Central Park area, still moving uptown, Ron saw that there was a glow in the street far ahead of them. The car seemed to be heading for the light. Soon Ron could see that there were lights—real street lights—ablaze along the streets. And people were walking along on the sidewalks. Shops were open, here and there. And every person he saw was black.

At last the car pulled up in front of a building that must have once been a church. The driver got out of the car and opened Ron's door.

"C'mon, whitey—shake it."

Ron slid out and stood on the sidewalk.

"Up this way," the driver said.

In the light of the street lamps, Ron could see that there were no people walking along this part of the sidewalk. A small crowd stood across the street, gawking at him. He shrugged and followed the driver. Ron noticed that the driver wore a sort of uniform of tight black slacks and black leather vest. Even his boots were black and highly shined. Ron felt shabby in his tattered old polyester suit and sandals. At least his clothes were black, also. Or they had once been. Now they were grimy and faded gray.

Inside the church they went. But it was no longer used as a church. The interior was long and narrow, with a high, sharply pointed ceiling and heavy old wood beams holding it together. Down on the wooden floor, benches and pews were gone. There were only a few folding chairs scattered around.

Up where the altar had once stood, there was a big carved wooden chair. Empty. Off to one side of it was a cluster of desks all pushed together. Four black guys sat there, their backs to Ron and his burly escort. They were talking to each other.

The driver nudged him, and Ron walked down the length of the church and up the three broad steps that led to the desks. Then he stood there, silently, waiting, while the blacks at the desks kept up their hushed conversation. Ron was just starting to wonder how long they'd keep him waiting, when one of the guys at the desks turned and noticed him.

"They got him," he said simply.

The others turned and looked at Ron. It was hard for Ron to tell what they were thinking. Three of the four were openly frowning. The fourth stood up and grinned.

He walked down the steps slowly toward Ron. He was tall, but very lean, spindly. His face was thin and bony. His eyes had a funny shape, almost oriental. His smile was wide, toothy. He looked friendly enough. He wore a simple outfit—vest, slacks, sandals—all sky-blue.

"They call me Timmy Jim," he said in a mild, slightly scratchy voice. "That ain't my real name, but it's what everybody calls me."

Ron blinked at the leader of the Muslims for a moment. "I'm Ron Morgan."

"I know. Know all about you. You got a good friend down in th' market—that ol' man Dewey. He got word to me you was in trouble. Tol' me I could use you. Says you're a freak with machines."

"I fix machines," Ron said.

Timmy Jim's grin got even bigger. "Okay. Great. You can fix 'em for the Muslims. More'n that, you teach some of my kids how to fix 'em."

Ron felt confused. "I didn't know the Muslims took in white people."

The grin vanished. "The Muslims do what I say. We ain't takin' you in as a member. We're gonna let you work here, *boy*.

We're savin' your ass—but only because that ol' man down in the market claims you can help us. If you ain't as good as he says you are, you're goin' right back where we got you. 'Stand?"

Ron heard himself say, "In other words, I'm a slave."

Timmy Jim's mouth dropped open. Then he broke into a wild, high-pitched cackling laugh. "Yeah, baby, that's just what you are!" He laughed and laughed. The others all laughed too.

Ron stood there, feeling their scorn bite into him. Then he thought about what Dino was going to do to him. *I don't really have a choice*, he realized.

It wasn't too bad. Most of the blacks treated him fairly. But they made it clear that he was white in a world where only black can be beautiful. The Muslims had many different shades of black, though. Some of them were the tannish brown of Latin Americans. Some were so deeply black that their skin shone with an African heat. Most were some shade between those two extremes. A few even looked like Indians.

There were more old people among the Muslims, although Ron saw little of them. Like Timmy Jim, most of the Muslim warriors were Ron's own age, or slightly older. The mechanics that Ron worked with were all in their early teens. Some of them resented taking orders from a white, but they did what Ron told them to with skill and speed.

Timmy Jim quickly set Ron up in the afternoons with even younger kids, whom he was expected to teach. They were fun. Young and eager and burning to learn about machinery. They learned fast. Ron soon had them fixing refrigerators and furnaces and even automobiles.

Once or twice some of the black warriors who always stayed near Ron gave him trouble. One guy clubbed Ron with a pistol butt once, for some reason that Ron never found out about. Two other warriors pulled him away, and Ron never saw that one again.

Timmy Jim himself was hard to figure out. Whenever Ron saw him, he seemed to be different. Sometimes he was quiet and friendly. Other times he seemed hard and mean. He could smile at Ron, talk pleasantly with him. Or he might call Ron "whitey," or "paleface," or "nigger's slave."

Slowly Ron began to understand. Timmy Jim was tough with him whenever there were other blacks watching. When they were alone, he was almost friendly.

As the weeks went by, Timmy Jim called Ron up to his private office more and more. It was in the building next to the old church. The office was bare, like a field general's tent. No decorations on the walls, except for a street map of Manhattan. No furniture, except a desk and its chair, plus a stiff wooden chair for a visitor.

"So tell me more about what it's like Outside," Timmy Jim would say.

Ron couldn't determine why he wanted to hear so much about the world outside the Dome. But he told Timmy Jim all about it, time after time.

"Wish you was back there, huh?" Timmy Jim asked Ron once.

"I guess so." Ron was surprised that he didn't feel more

strongly about it. His parents, his friends, his whole life was Outside. But that was so long ago, so far away. It felt strange even to think about it. As if that life belonged to somebody else, some other kid, not Ron himself.

The winter passed slowly. Ron lived in a single small room in a building that had once been a school. In fact, it was a school once again, because the Muslims used its large downstairs rooms for Ron's "classes" in mechanical repair. At least once a week, Timmy Jim had Ron up to his office to talk about the world Outside. The rest of the time Ron spent teaching the kids how to fix machines, or how to build new machines. He hardly did any fixing on his own now.

Ron taught, he worked, he ate, he slept. Outside of the kids he was teaching, and Timmy Jim, the only other people he knew were the young warriors who never let him far out of their sight and a few of the girls who brought him his two meals each day. He had struck up a conversational acquaintance with one of the girls, an olive-skinned Puerto Rican named Liana.

But Ron's only real amusement was his weekly visit with Timmy Jim. The Muslim leader was relaxed and happy when Ron saw him; they shared sandwiches and drinks each visit. Gradually, as the weeks turned into months, Ron began to see that Timmy Jim was always asking questions about the weapons that the police Outside carried, what the roads were like, how electric cars operated, how many police each Tract had, where the Army bases were located.

Then one afternoon, as Ron sat in that stiff-backed chair in front of Timmy Jim's desk and talked about the turbo-train system, it all clicked into place.

"You're going to invade the Outside!"

Timmy Jim laughed. "Been wonderin' how long it'd take you to tumble to it."

"But that's crazy! You can't—"

"Sure I can't. Not now. Got to take over all th' gangs under the Dome first. That'll take a few more years. We start next fall, soon's the gates close down after the summer season. Then we hit the gangs between here'n the market. Gonna be tough making white gangs see things our way, but in four to five years we'll have every gang under the Dome workin' together—all under one leader. Me."

Ron felt staggered. "And then?"

"Then Outside. That's where all the real loot is . . . that's where we're goin'."

"My God."

Timmy Jim leaned forward in his chair and pointed at Ron. "See . . . the only way I can keep all the black gangs together is t' make 'em dream of takin' over the whole City. The only way I'll be able to make *all* the gangs work together without killin' each other *is* to turn 'em loose on the Outside."

"But it'll never work," Ron answered. "There's hundreds of millions of people out there."

"Just more loot, that's all."

"And the police . . ."

"We can handle 'em."

"The Army . . ."

Timmy Jim smiled. "Yeah. The Army. You wanna know somethin'? Half the spades in the Army are Muslims. We planted 'em. You just watch your Army when we go Outside. Just watch what they do."

Ron sat there, open-mouthed. Timmy Jim laughed.

It took weeks for the idea to sink in. Ron thought about it every day. *Conquer the Outside. He's crazy!* But still the idea scared him.

The weather grew warmer. A new batch of kids was given to Ron for training. The youngsters he had started with left the area, and he never saw them again. *Where did Timmy Jim send them?* he wondered. *And why?*

There were reports of battles, skirmishes along the borders of Muslim territory. One whole white gang was wiped out when Timmy Jim decided to attack it in real force. The border fighting stopped after that.

And then, on a warm day in late spring, Sylvia showed up.

**R**on was working. He had a large classroom filled with kids aged ten to fifteen. Big windows let the daylight in. The glass had been smashed out of them long ago. There were about forty kids, all bent over little electric motors or transistor radios that the Muslims had dug up for Ron to use in class. The kids worked quietly, while Ron fidgeted up at the front of the room. It was warm, springtime, the time of year when school should be ending and you could go outdoors for baseball and picnics and . . .

A pair of armed guards appeared at the classroom door. *Trouble*, thought Ron.

He went out to the door and stepped into the hallway. Sylvia was there.

He felt his heart stop for a moment. She looked older, very tired. Her blouse and shorts were grimy and wrinkled, her face smudged with dirt. But she was still beautiful.

Ron wanted to reach out and take her in his arms and hold her forever. Instead he did nothing.

"Hello Ron."

It took him two tries to find his voice. "Hello."

"I . . . I wanted t' see you," she said slowly, softly. "They let me come here, but only for a coupla minutes. They're gonna take me right back again."

"Back to where?"

"Gramercy turf. Frankie's puttin' th' gang back t'gether again. We got about twenny kids . . . there'll be more . . ."

"What's Dino doing?"

"He's dead."

"Dead?"

She nodded. "Chelsea guys did it. He got inna fight with their chief. I tried t' do it myself a coupla times, but I couldn't work up th' nerve." Her eyes looked haunted, tortured. "He got what he deserved."

Ron put a hand on her shoulder, but there was nothing he could say.

"They treatin' you okay here?" Sylvia asked.

"Yes. And you—are you all right? Is there anything I can—"

"I'm okay." She tried to smile. "Don' worry about me. I can take care o' myself."

"Yeah."

"Well . . . I gotta go back now. I jes' wanted t' see ya and letcha know Dino's dead. If they ever letcha get back t' Gramercy . . . an' . . . well, I'm sorry about everything. If it wasn't fer me, you'd be Outside now, back home . . . I'm sorry, Ron."

"It wasn't your fault. It's all right."

"Oh . . . here." She fumbled in the pocket of her shorts. "Here's some stuff Dino took off ya, that first time."

Ron took the things from her hand. A house key. A credit card. His ID card.

*My ID card!* He glanced up sharply at Sylvia. She knew! She knew she had just handed him the key to freedom. Ron looked over at the two warriors. They were loafing against the wall, talking to each other.

"Good luck, Ron," Sylvia said. "And thanks."

"No, wait!" he whispered fiercely. "Hold on. We can both get out. When the gates open . . ."

She shook her head, smiling sadly. "Ron . . . no way. We'd never make it t'gether. You're what you are an' I'm what I am. There's no way fer us t' make it t'gether."

"But . . ."

She kissed him lightly on the lips, then turned and started to walk away, down the hall. The two black warriors followed after her. Ron stood rooted to the spot, holding the key and cards in his outstretched hand.

"Sylvia!" he called. But she didn't turn around. She just kept walking.


For more than a week, Ron's mind was in a turmoil. *How can I get away, with them watching me all the time? And how can I leave Sylvia here?* That was the real question. No matter how hard he thought about it, he knew that she was right. There was no way to bring her Outside.

Could he get himself Outside?

The springtime passed slowly. The weather warmed. The summer began and the gates opened to let the visitors in for the vacation season.

"The tourists never come up here," Timmy Jim said, "The hardtops make sure of that."

And Timmy Jim made sure that Ron didn't get out of Muslim territory. He always felt the eyes of warriors on him. Even at night.

But finally Ron made a break for freedom. He waited until very late one night, several weeks after the summer season had started. His sleeping quarters had been moved to an old hotel building, where there were warriors sleeping in all the rooms around him. More guards were on duty all night down in the hotel lobby.

Ron had studied the building very carefully. He didn't go down the stairs to the lobby. He forced open the doors to one of the old elevator shafts.

For a moment he stood at the edge of the open doorway, staring into the darkness of the shaft. There was emptiness waiting for him, and a five-story drop to the bottom. Ron took a deep breath, then leaped out into the dark emptiness, reaching for the steel cable that hung in the middle of the shaft, hoping he could grab it, praying that it would hold his weight.

It was slimy with grease. Ron felt his breath puff out of him as his body slammed into the cable. His hands slid and scraped, but held. The cable's creaking, as his body swayed on it, seemed loud enough to wake everybody in the building.

For a moment Ron hung there. But only for a moment. Slowly, painfully, he started to climb up the cable. It was difficult. The cable was slippery. Finally, though, he had climbed the six flights to the equipment shed on the roof.

*Wonder why they never asked me to fix the elevators?* Ron asked himself as he stepped out of the shed and onto the roof.

He crossed one roof after another until he was at the end of the block. Then he went downstairs inside the building, knowing that it was empty and unguarded. He made it to the street and started walking.

Dawn was already starting to brighten the new day when Ron stopped on the sidewalk next to the last row of buildings before the huge girders of the Dome. Across the wide avenue ahead of him, the massive steel girders reared and arched so far overhead that they were lost in haze. And on the other side of the Dome— freedom? *No*, Ron realized. *Not freedom. Just another kind of world, with its own kind of slavery.*

Still, Ron started walking along that avenue, following the curving flank of the Dome, looking for the nearest gate. As he walked block after block, it began to get brighter with daylight. The streets were still empty, though.

Off to his left, just a few blocks away was Central Park. Ron kept a careful eye out for stray dogs. He had heard from the Muslims that the dog packs sent out scouts, and a single dog's bark could bring out a snarling horde in no time.

By mid-morning, he saw a bus growling along one of the

crosstown streets several blocks up ahead of him. He walked faster. Soon he saw well-dressed people strolling on the streets, staring up at the buildings and the overspanning Dome. Tourists! A gate must be nearby.

As he walked among the strolling visitors, they stared at his filthy clothes and ragged looks and skirted clear of him. Ron laughed and clutched the credit card in his pocket. He went to the first hotel he could find. Using his credit card on the automated registration desk, he obtained a room and ordered new clothes. He bathed for an hour, feeling the beautiful hot water and clean-smelling soap take away his dirt and pain. And his fear.

For the first time in nearly a year, Ron wasn't afraid.

But as he dressed, he began to worry about Sylvia. And Dewey. Maybe she was right, and there was no place Outside for her. But what about the old man? *I can't leave him here to go blind, all by himself.* Yet, if he tried to take Dewey through a gate with him, Ron knew that the guards would send the ID-less old man to the Tombs.

He dressed slowly, lost in his thoughts, pulling on a disposable green zipsuit almost exactly like the one he had worn when he'd first come to the City. He was pushing his feet into the new boots when his hotel room door swung open and Timmy Jim walked in.

The fear flashed through Ron again. He stood there on the soft carpeting, fresh and clean, dressed in a crisp new suit. But he felt the way he had felt all year long, as if anything could happen to him any minute. He was alone. Unprotected.

Two black warriors stood out in the hall, grim-faced. Timmy Jim shut the door quietly.

"Where do you think you're goin'?" he asked.

"Outside. I'm getting out."

"You think so."

"Now look," Ron said, "you can't start trouble in here. The police . . ."

Timmy Jim smiled, but there was no humor in it. "The hardtops been paid off. I can take this hotel apart, brick by brick, if I want to. I can take this whole friggin' *City* apart, any time I want to!"

Ron sank down on the bed. "Okay, so you're top man. But there's one thing you can't do."

"Name it."

"You can't make me go back with you. I'm finished. I'm going Outside . . . or you'll have to kill me. One or the other."

Timmy Jim blinked at him. "You're bluffin'."

"No, I'm not."

"You think you're gonna go Outside and warn 'em that we're comin' out . . . that we're gonna take over?"

Ron shrugged.

Laughing, Timmy Jim said, "Man, they won't believe word number one! They'll think you're spaced out!"

"Then you've got nothing to worry about."

"I saved your ass, man," Timmy Jim snapped. "You owe me your *life*. You ain't gonna get outta that."

Ron answered, "I trained nearly a hundred kids for you. They know as much as I do. Let them train others. You got your money's worth out of me."

The smile crept back across Timmy Jim's bony face. "Tired of bein' a slave, huh?"

Ron nodded.

"Can't say I blame you." Timmy Jim walked over to the window and pushed the curtain aside to look down at the street for a few moments. Then, turning to Ron, he said, "Lemme tell you somethin'. When they shut down New York City . . . when they officially called it closed and evacuated everybody . . . they didn't let us out."

Ron looked up at him. "Us?"

"The blacks," Timmy Jim said. "The Puerto Ricans. The poor people in the ghettos in Harlem and the upper West Side and all. They didn't let any of 'em out."

"The City was evacutated, emptied," Ron said. "The only people who stayed were like Dewey, people who hid out until they declared the City officially closed."

"Bullshit. Oh, they took out the whites, all right. Rich and poor. Irish and Italian and WASP and all. They got out okay. But they kept *us* inside. When we tried to get out, they beat us back with clubs, electric prods, water cannon, lasers—they didn't let us out, man! They closed this City and wrote it off as a dead loss and claimed all of us were dead."

"No, that can't be . . ."

"It sure as hell was," Timmy Jim said, his fists clenched at his sides. "That was *why* they closed the City down, man. The real reason! Wrote off all the welfare cases. Officially they no longer exist. One touch of the computer's tape and *poof!* all them records erased."

Ron couldn't believe it. "They left you here?"

"They left us here, baby. Left us to starve, to freeze, to be rat bait. They left us to fight with each other and kill ourselves off."

"Holy God."

"God's got nothin' to do with it," Timmy Jim answered. "Anyway, don't you know He's black?" He smiled ruefully.

"Is this really true? They closed the City to get rid of you?" Ron asked.

Timmy Jim nodded. "That's why the Muslims took charge. We had to get some organization. Had to figure out how to *live*, man. There was some people Outside who was willing to give us a little help. Smugglin' in food, stuff like that. But it was nowhere near enough. No way. Not even the black market was enough. But we managed. We survived."

"And now . . ."

"And now, instead of fightin' each other, all the Muslim brothers are united. We fight the white gangs. That keeps us together. In a few more years, *all* the gangs will be together."

"United by your plan to invade the Outside."

"That's right."

"And you're afraid I'm going to warn them, out there," Ron said.

"Go warn 'em," Timmy Jim said, standing in front of Ron. "Go tell 'em everything I just told you. They won't believe you. They won't lissen to you. Not 'til it's too late."

"I can go?" Ron asked.

"Yeah . . . go. Go. I set you free, whitey. Just like Lincoln. Go on Outside and tell 'em all about us. Won't do you any good. They won't believe you. Not 'til they see us comin'. And we *will* be comin'. That's a promise."

Timmy Jim walked past Ron to the door, opened it, and left. Ron sat there on the edge of the bed, unmoving.

"Not to warn them, Jim," he said to the empty room. "To *change* them. I'm going back Outside to change them. They know the City exists. They know the kids are in here, in this jungle, turning into animals. They know it, but they ignore it. So I'm going to change them. I'm going to rub their noses in the filth they've left behind them, just as my face has been rubbed in it for the past year. I'm going to make them listen, make them realize. I'll break all the patterns. I'll change everything and everybody. I'll break their Career vectors and their curfews and their endless Tracts. Even if I have to make myself President, I'll make them change. They can't let the cities fester like this. They can't do this to *people!* It's like a cancer. We've got to cure it or it will kill us all."

Finally understanding what he had to do, Ron strode out of the hotel and down to the gate. He pushed through the swarms of people flocking into the City for a vacation good-time. In his mind's eye he saw Dewey, saw Sylvia, and little Davey and Al. Even Dino. And Timmy Jim, dark and powerful, ready to change the world *his* way.

At the gate, the white-helmeted police guard looked at Ron strangely as he showed his ID. Ron knew that he was thinner than the photo on the card. There were lines in his face that had never been there before. Finally the hardtop handed the ID back to him.

"You're leaving? But the fun's just getting started."

"Yes," Ron said. "I know."